C000050318

A Telling Time

By
Glynnis Hayward

PublishAmerica
Baltimore

First printing

ISBN: 1-59129-591-2
PUBLISHED BY PUBLISHAMERICA BOOK PUBLISHERS
www.publishamerica.com
Baltimore

Printed in the United States of America

For my parents, Neville and Audrey,
who taught me to look up and see the stars.

ACKNOWLEDGMENTS

First and foremost, I thank my brother Terry, who inspired me with his ideas and ideals, as well as his work both as an attorney and an Anglican priest. His writings were the catalyst for the book. I express special thanks to Brian, my husband, whose insight was invaluable as he patiently listened, read, edited and made suggestions. Thanks also to my daughter, Lindsay, for her cover design, and to my son, Graham, for his technical help.

My appreciation extends to Iain Burns for his objective support and encouragement, and to the many friends who, over the years, have urged me on. I am grateful to Archbishop Emeritus Desmond Tutu, for giving his permission to be quoted in this book.

All characters in the book are entirely fictional.

PROLOGUE

It was the siren's sudden blast, right behind her, that jolted Helen back from her thoughts to where she was - driving Highway 17 on autopilot. Immediately she could feel her heart pounding. Pulling over carefully, she braced as the CHP officer climbed out of his patrol car and strode briskly towards her. She bit her bottom lip as he approached, noting how he rolled his shoulders and fingered the gun at his side, before glaring in the window and demanding to see her driver's license. He waited with one hand on his hip, the other on her car, cleared his throat and added gruffly, "I need to see your insurance and car registration too."

Helen's hands were shaking as she scratched in the glove compartment and her purse for the documents. She turned off the CD, but her heartbeat sounded like a heavy bass that continued to play while the officer waited. Taking the papers from her without a word, he strode back to his patrol car so that he could run a DMV check. This was the first time she had been pulled over in the eighteen years that she had lived in California, and her last dealings with police, in her native South Africa, had been traumatic. Her eyes were fixed on the gun slung to his hip, dark and menacing. She felt panic rising in her chest as he returned to her car and peered inside.

"Do you know what speed you were doing?" he demanded.

She shook her head and swallowed hard.

"You don't know. Let me ask you something else. Do you know what the speed limit is?"

"Sixty-five," she acknowledged in a tight voice.

"Correct." He drummed his fingers on the roof of her car. "You were doing eighty-one miles per hour."

"I didn't realize I was going that fast, Officer. I'm sorry. I'm late for an appointment and I wasn't concentrating."

"That's real dangerous. The most important rule when you're driving is to be alert. You've got to know what's going on around you. You didn't even see my lights flashing behind you." He stared hard at her. "I'll have to cite you for this." Without another word he proceeded to write her up and then handed her the ticket with a polite nod. "Concentrate on the driving now and get on your way." He half-smiled as he turned and strolled back to his distinctive, black and white car.

She looked at the piece of paper and it felt so inconsequential compared to the anxiety she had been pre-programmed to feel. Her hands were shaking as she started to laugh and cry at the same time. "Is that all? This is so civilized," she thought, restarting her car. "I mean it's a damn nuisance, and I suppose I'll have to go to Traffic School, but it's civilized!" She shook her head in disbelief, making sure she stuck to the speed limit, but it was difficult keeping her thoughts from straying to her upcoming South African trip - and the policemen she had known there.

She was finally going to testify before the Truth and Reconciliation Committee. It hadn't been an easy decision because it re-opened such painful, terrifying memories. So many years had passed since all the horror, and so many people involved were dead. It was hard, even now, to accept that she would never again see her father, or David Marais.

Her present preoccupation had started ten days ago when she was woken by the clatter of the fax machine. She remembered sitting up sharply in bed, cursing at the unblinking, red digits on the alarm - 3:17 am. "Damn. Must be from South Africa. It's almost lunchtime there." Tempting as it was to roll over and ignore the intrusion, telephones and faxes in the night always compelled her to answer their demands, and she hastened to do so again.

"We need to turn the bloody ringer off that machine. It's enough . to wake the dead. I bet that's Pat Moodley planning his trip to California," Al lay grumbling next to her. "Mm-hm, I can see the letterhead from here, Moodley and Ngcobo. Can't they just e-mail us?"

"I can't read it without my glasses - what's it say?" She handed the fax to her husband, mumbling, "If it's not an emergency, I'm going back to sleep." Then she quickly added, "He is okay isn't he?"

Al's response was an involuntary intake of air. Now fully awake, he murmured, "Well, well, well," while staring at the page. "You're not going to believe this, Mrs. Griffin. We'd better pack our bags, we've got a plane to catch!"

"What's going on? I thought he was coming here?"

"Nope! Looks like we're going there, a.s.a.p. Those bastards Erasmus and Van Zyl have applied to the Truth and Reconciliation Committee for amnesty. They appear next week."

Suddenly Helen felt cold and transfixed by the mention of their names. Her chest constricted as she grabbed hold of the bed, steadying herself from the shock wave of painful memories. It had been twenty-six years, yet she could still remember her body collapsing at the feet of those monsters, and hear her skull shatter as they kicked her. Though not proven, she knew they were to blame. Fingering the deep scars in her scalp, she recalled the slow, painful struggle to live a normal life again after six months of plastic surgery and rehabilitation. Hatred had formed a festering growth in her brain that refused to be cauterized.

Al gently put his arms around her. "Sweetheart, Pat would like you to testify. I know its something you would rather forget, but he believes your appearance could help prove they were criminals. One word from you would convince anyone that their actions had no political justification." He cupped her face in his hands reassuringly, "But if it's too painful, forget the idea, because your happiness is the most important thing." He kissed her forehead, adding quickly, "They can send those two to hell as far as I'm concerned, and the quicker the ride the better."

She stared at him a long time. "This is the moment that I suppose I've always wanted. But now that it's here, I feel so afraid."

He pulled her towards him in a protective embrace, and she buried her head in his chest. "They might get away with saying that the letter bomb sent to Dave was politically motivated," she muttered under her breath. Looking up at her husband, she said in measured tones, "but *I know* they planted that car bomb to kill my Dad, and I know why. That wasn't politics: they did it to save their own skins. They did it to stop him from testifying before the investigation." She was shouting, and anger seemed to drain her energy as she sunk into the bed with a sigh. The silence was heavy and uncomfortable while she stared at a place on the ceiling as if it were ten thousand miles away. The demons that still visited her in the dead of night moved into her consciousness. Thinking of the nights when she awoke screaming, Al gently rubbed her shoulders.

She turned to him with tears welling in her eyes, swallowed hard, and in a very strained voice, whispered, "I can't do it Al. I know I should, but I just can't cope with all of that again."

"That's fine, my angel. Don't worry about it. There's a hell of a lot of other stuff to nail them with. It wasn't just you and your Dad they hurt you know! And if you aren't up to it, I don't want you doing it either. I'll e-mail Pat tomorrow and tell him. They can get plenty of other witnesses - no doubt Philemon will be there. Who could have more to say than him? And I'm happy to go and let those bastards have it. Come," he said, taking her in his arms, "let's try and get some more sleep."

Helen tossed and turned, feeling anxiety squeeze her heart in a vice. She cried softly into her pillow; tears of frustration, rage and grief, while Al lay pretending he was asleep, at a loss to comfort her.

Yet sometimes, however much we try to bury the past, the past will not allow this to happen. It was about a week later when she turned on CNN that she heard the newscaster say, "In South Africa today, six white policemen were suspended from duty pending investigation of a video that has surfaced. The following scenes are graphic and viewer discretion is recommended." Helen stopped in her tracks, watching the screen with horror as it showed six white policemen releasing a team of vicious dogs on a group of terrified, illegal immigrants. These black men were desperately trying to protect their faces and genitalia, as laughter was heard in the background.

She froze, staring at the T.V. long after the news had finished, but hearing nothing. She was still standing there when Al came in and she turned to him, trancelike. "Have you heard the news about South Africa today?"

Gritting his teeth, he nodded.

"Those monsters are still using the same old tactics and they think they can get away with it. They think they're above the law. I'm going back, Al. I'm going to prove what they did to my father. If I don't testify, there's more chance that they'll walk away with amnesty granted to them. How soon can we leave?"

****

The fifteen-hour flight from J.F.K., New York to Johannesburg International is one of the longest commercial flights in the world. Add to that the five-hour flight from San Francisco and this could hardly be called a pleasure trip. The Griffins settled into their seats and prepared for take-off.

Listening to the strangely familiar accents of the South African Airways flight crew, brought a wave of warmth to Helen. She looked at Al and they smiled. Pride was a new sensation that they were still getting used to feeling about South Africa, with its bright new flag and newfound tolerance. She remembered the shame they had felt when they left that hot, sad, day eighteen years ago: a shame that compelled them to leave rather than raise their new baby in the land of his birth.

So much had changed in the intervening years. It was hard to believe that the government of South Africa could change without civil war, although much blood had flowed; and who would have thought that the imprisoned, exiled and banned would now be in the government. Their friend, Philemon Dlamini, had been released from Robben Island in 1993, after serving nineteen years on that godforsaken piece of land that lay so tantalizingly close to Cape Town. He was now a cabinet minister in the new government and a revered elder statesman. It still seemed like a fairytale to Helen. And that frightened young boy, Simon Gumede, who had come knocking on their door one morning: after training at the London School of Economics during his exile from South Africa, he was now an assistant to the Minister of Finance.

She wished at times that they had remained to be part of the new South Africa, instead of emigrating. When something is ingrained in your being, it doesn't fade easily. She glanced over at her son and daughter, engrossed in the movie. They were intrigued by their South African heritage, but removed from it. It was gratifying to her though, that they had a real love and understanding of their roots, albeit with no desire to return to them.

Homesickness can be crippling, even terminal. She winced at the memory of the farewells when they had left, their parents all valiantly fighting back tears--even offering support, whilst disapproving of their children's decision. Her close friend Mary had always said that the first baby would heal all the wounds, and she had been correct. The grandparents from either side of the family were at last amiable to one another, even attempting to speak each other's language. What pain she and Al had caused, taking away the adored new grandchild to the farthest end of the earth, where the loneliness on arrival was worse than she could ever have imagined.

Her thoughts were interrupted by a dark, smiling face offering her some orange juice. Miriam Chiya's name was printed on her elegant flight attendant's uniform. They smiled at one another and Helen thought that the advertisement lived up to its promise; this was Africa's warmest welcome! As she sipped her juice she felt a flush of pride. Reaching over to Al, she squeezed his hand and whispered, "Tell me I'm not dreaming. It doesn't seem real."

"It's no dream, it's the New South Africa. You're going home, H.A." He squeezed her hand in return. "It's a good feeling, and you've got an important job to do there, setting the record straight."

She frowned and said, "Sometimes I'm not sure this Truth and Reconciliation is a good thing. I mean, what's the logic? Just because someone tells the truth to the Commission and says they're sorry, all is forgiven? Sort of, come to confession and have a clean slate for next week!"

"Mm, I hear what you say," agreed Al, " but remember, it's aimed at reconciliation. It's part of the reconstruction process. You know the theory that before there can be mercy, there has to be justice. Who knows, maybe you'll be able to find some peace too, my love. I really hope so." He caressed her cheek softly and then added, "I believe that the old priest who was on the Kwa Mashu Committee is now on the Commission in Durban. Maybe we'll see him."

"I remember seeing him in court once." She sighed, "I don't know how I'll survive this flight, I can't wait to get back now."

"Oh, have a few glasses of wine and watch the movie. You'll be sleeping like a baby before long. Just don't snore!"

"You're a fine one to talk," she laughed, "but you can wake me if I do."

Helen's thoughts could not focus on the movie. Long-suppressed memories of her life almost thirty years ago kept flooding into her mind. Finally, she allowed herself to close her eyes and let her thoughts recollect those people, places and voices from a different time. Slowly the whole, terrible story unfolded itself to her again as if she were detached, watching herself and all the others....

Chapter 1

Durban, South Africa, 1973. Philemon Dlamini tried to shut out the scene before him, but he'd been here so many times before that it was indelibly etched on his eyelids. Besides which, the stench of sweaty fear from inmates, crammed into the stark cell, reminded him that he was back in prison for being on the street without a pass. His eyes opened quickly at the sound of a familiar, distasteful voice, and focused on a man he knew as Toughy, surrounded by his followers.

Toughy always reminded Philemon of a hyena, with his nervous laugh and predatory ways. Once again he had found a victim who was already crushed by the power of the police, but was now also terrified by the pack of scavengers around him. The young man, hardly more than a boy, crouched on the floor hugging his knees as the Hyena shouted, "Two rand! That's what you must pay to sleep here tonight."

"But I'm poor," the boy protested, "I can't pay you. I've only got two rand and I must send it to my mother, otherwise she'll starve."

Philemon intervened with a roar. "You will not take this young man's money." Turning his head towards the boy, he said, "Sit in the corner behind me and don't move." He turned again to glare at

Toughy, adding, "Now if anyone wants his money they must get past me first." He stood tall and firm, with his fists clenched and muscles flexed.

The Hyena hesitated, intimidated by Philemon's size and wrath. Sensing this, his followers slowly retreated until Toughy was left standing alone. In disgust he spat on the floor and cursed. Without taking his eyes off his foe, Philemon backed up and sank to his haunches next to the frightened young man.

"I greet you, my brother," he said. "My name is Philemon Dlamini."

"Thank you my brother, I'm Simon Gumede."

"Why are you here?" asked the older man.

"I'm not sure. The policeman said it was because I don't have a passbook, but that's not true. I do have one at the hostel where I stay in Kwa Mashu."

"The laws of the white man are strange and you'll have to learn them to survive here, Simon. You have to carry your passbook with you always. That's the law." He put his hand on the young man's shoulder and said, "As you learn the ways of the city, don't grow like that Hyena there. He always preys on other people's hardships. It's very hard to be black, don't make it harder. That man is bad."

"Why don't the police stop him? They heard him shouting at me, but they walked away. Are they afraid of him?"

"Oh no, they're not afraid because we're locked up. They don't care what happens to you tonight - or tomorrow."

"What will happen tomorrow?" Simon shot Philemon an anxious look.

"They'll take us to court in the back of a van, and we'll be charged with not having our passbooks."

"But I do have one," said Simon. "I keep telling everyone. I do have a pass but I left it at the hostel. I can get it and show them."

"They don't care Simon. The law says you must carry it with you. Listen to me carefully. When the prosecutor charges you tomorrow, tell him you're guilty and very sorry. Then he'll fine you ten rand or send you to prison for five days. If you say anything else, he'll send you to prison for ten days because he doesn't want to listen to your story."

Simon shook his head with a heavy sigh. "I don't understand. It doesn't make any sense."

"Trust me, Simon. It doesn't make sense, just do as I say."

"What else can I do?" he groaned. " Thanks my brother, you've helped me twice already in one night. I trust you."

"Good. Now try and sleep a little. Tomorrow will be hard."

They both slept fitfully and were already awake next morning when a guard banged on the bars with metal cups, which were then thrown on the floor, followed by two buckets. One of these contained a thin gruel for the prisoners to eat, while the other had water for drinking or washing. As Simon stood up and stretched his cramped limbs, he saw a third bucket steaming in the middle of the room, over which someone stood urinating. He understood now why the room stank, and he longed to be back on the farm again. He wished he could feel the cool breeze that rustled through the tall gum trees, and smell the pungent eucalyptus. He thought about his little cousins laughing and chattering as they played a mock stick fight. Sometimes they forgot to herd the goats as they played, and then his aunt or mother would come shouting up the hill. It seemed so far away.

Philemon had no stomach for the food. He left the others to fight over the gruel and dipped his hands into the water bucket. After drinking thirstily from his cupped hands, he wiped his face and watched Simon sadly as the young man surveyed his surroundings. "Another life will never be the same," he mused.

It seemed to Simon that the cell looked even smaller in the morning light than it had the night before. The ceiling was fly-spotted and the whitewashed walls were covered in graffiti. About twenty people were crammed together trying to get turns with the various buckets, whose contents spilled over onto the concrete floor. Suddenly armed guards entered the area outside the cell with loud shouts, and stood at intervals around the walls. One of them opened the door and ordered the prisoners to follow. Simon felt a hand on his arm and looked up to see Philemon walking next to him. It was a comfort to have such a self-assured friend.

They were all herded into a large courtyard where police vans were parked with their back doors wide open, ready to receive the damned into the gates of hell. They were ordered to climb inside and then the doors were slammed shut and locked. As they jolted forward the noise became deafening with shouted obscenities from prisoners who were being roughly thrown against each other. They drove in convoy, like tumbrels to the guillotine, with passers-by staring silently and uncomfortably. As they screeched to a stop at a traffic light, Simon heard women's voices singing in beautiful harmony from one of the other vans. Philemon turned to him and said loudly, so as to be heard above the din, "Listen to the words. Those are songs our people used to sing when they went to battle."

"We should fight again. There are so few of them and so many of us, what are we waiting for?" Simon shouted back.

"Not now. They're too strong for us." The van lurched forward again and Philemon shouted even louder for Simon to hear. "Our leaders plead for us to own our land again, and have our families live with us. But they put our leaders on Robben Island for asking these things." He shook his head and muttered, "How can they make a man live away from his family?"

"But how can our leaders lead, if they're in prison? It doesn't make any sense. We should fight to get them out," replied Simon. There was no time to answer, however, as the vans lurched to the left and came to an abrupt stop outside the courthouse.

Amidst screamed orders and abuse, the prisoners were crammed into a holding cell, surrounded by armed guards who stood with their guns slung menacingly from their shoulders, ready to fire.

"What happens now?" whispered Simon nervously.

"When it's your turn, they'll call your name and push you through that gate. You'll go down a passage and then you'll be shoved into court. That's where the magistrate will be. He'll sentence you to prison or fine you."

Simon quickly answered, "You know I can't pay."

"Then you'll go to prison and serve your sentence. Be brave

Simon," the older man said patiently. "You survived last night so you know you can survive again. You'll lose your job, for sure, but when you get out of prison, go to this address." He handed him a scrap of paper. "That's where I stay. I'll help you to find another job and I want you to help me with some other very important work."

Simon felt a little more confident. "What work?" he asked.

"I'll tell you later. It's nine o'clock now and time for the court to start its business. Be a proud Zulu, Simon. Don't let them make you cry."

One by one the prisoners were called and disappeared through the gate with monotonous regularity. Long after Philemon had been summoned, Simon was called and joined the shuffling line to court. Once there, he was led to the dock by a policeman and found himself staring at a small, bald man dressed in a black gown, sitting behind a desk.

"Simon Gumede, you are charged with the crime that on or about the fourth day of June, 1973, and in the city of Durban, you did wrongfully and unlawfully fail to produce your passbook to a police officer on demand. Do you plead guilty or not guilty?"

Simon stared blankly, looking for the owner of the voice. He heard it again, saying impatiently, "Do you plead guilty or not guilty? Come on boy, we haven't got all day."

He located the source. It was a tall man with a thick mustache, also wearing a black gown.

"Not guilty," replied Simon quickly. Then remembering his friend's advice he corrected himself. "I mean I'm guilty my boss. I'm very sorry, I mean guilty."

"You are accordingly found guilty," intoned the magistrate behind the desk. "Is there anything you wish to say before I sentence you?"

Philemon's advice was forgotten in confusion as Simon pleaded, "Yes my boss. There's my mother and I must send her money. If I go to prison she'll starve because I'll lose my job."

"Slow down and calm yourself," reprimanded the magistrate. "I have to write down what you say."

"Yes, my boss," replied Simon, and then started to speak again faster than before. "I do have a passbook. It's at the hostel. I can show you, please my boss. My mother...."

"Yes, yes, your mother will starve. I've heard enough. Everybody's mother is going to starve if I were to believe all I hear in this court. I haven't seen too much evidence of starving mothers. You're repeating yourself and wasting the court's time. I sentence you to a fine of twenty rand or ten days in prison."

As he stood in the dock staring disbelievingly at the magistrate, a policeman pushed Simon out the door and into a waiting police van. He desperately tried to stop sobs escaping from his clenched jaw when, through a watery film of tears, he saw the large shape of his friend.

"Philemon," he cried, "I forgot to take your advice and I made the magistrate angry. You were right, he sentenced me to ten days."

"I also got ten days."

"Why?" asked Simon aghast, "Did you also forget?"

"No," grunted the older man. "Oh no. You see this was not my first offence, so the magistrate wasn't lenient with me. Be strong now, Simon, be a man. You're a proud Zulu." He patted him. "From now on I'll protect you and teach you like my own son."

Simon regained his composure under this steadying influence. "Yes," he agreed, "and I won't let you down again. I promise."

Philemon felt his chest tighten with emotion as he put his arm around the sixteen year old. He thought longingly of his own small son, Nkosinati, at home in Zululand, and he wondered bitterly whether this same fate lay ahead for him too. His grip tightened with determination on Simon's shoulder. "We'll change things, my friend. Life is not going to be poverty, passes and prison forever. You and my son will be free men."

Chapter 2

Durban is a busy port on the east coast of South Africa. Its humid heat is sometimes cooled by sea breezes that sway arched palm fronds in a graceful dance along the Esplanade. People lie here enjoying relief from the heat, dozing on the grassy embankments and listening to crackling radios. All the while, the Indian Ocean rolls to shore with a continual, soporific beat, and colorful rickshaws take passengers on short rides, dipping, lifting and high kicking. Queen Victoria stands serenely, holding her scepter and orb, surveying these people who are no longer her subjects, while pigeons sit disrespectfully on her head and shoulders. Twice a day on weekdays, however, the genial atmosphere erupts into a sinister battle. Rush hour!

In the late afternoon madness of Smith Street, two young attorneys walked to their cars, deep in conversation. They were oblivious of the busy pedestrian traffic bumping around them, or the honking of cars and buses as they switched lanes and raced to traffic lights. Alan Griffin, the taller of the two, sauntered along kicking at cigarette butts and bottle tops that littered the street. His leather briefcase swung in one hand like a large pendulum, stopping occasionally while the other hand tucked in a transgressant shirttail. David Marais, six inches shorter, strode earnestly to keep abreast.

"Come around to my place tonight if you can," said David excitedly. "I've got to tell you and Helen my idea."

"Can't you give me a clue now?" laughed Al.

"Maybe, but you really need to hear the whole story. Let me just say this, I've figured a way to screw the whole passbook system." He looked furtively over his shoulder and added, "It's so obvious you won't believe how simple it can be!"

"Yeah, right," said Al. "The pass laws are the bones of Apartheid and you've figured a way to screw that up very simply! How in hell's name are you going to do that?"

"It's quite within the law. We'll do what we're trained to do, we'll defend them."

David paused and studied his friend's face carefully. "Do you get what I'm saying?"

"No, can't say I do. Tell me more," said Al.

"Those poor bastards pass through court like an assembly line. Each case takes about three minutes. All we need to do is slow the process down and we'll overload the courts. They can't cope now, but we could make them groan with the weight."

"Dave, that sounds great, but be realistic. How many of those cases pass through court each day? How are you and I going to defend them all and still carry our share of the workload as partners of a law firm? We have to pay the bills at the end of the month you know."

"I've got an idea. Come around tonight and let me explain."

"Okay, sure. This I can't wait to hear. I'm afraid you're going to have a skeptical audience."

"Hey, what kind of attorney are you, prejudging without hearing all the facts?"

"All right," he agreed, hearing the indignation in Dave's voice, "I know you've got something brewing, we'll come and listen to your plan." By now they'd reached the parking garage. "See you later then, after dinner."

Berea Road was a frenzy of diesel fumes and noise as Alan made his way home amidst the crazy exodus from the city. Slowly he weaved and dodged up to Ridge Road, and noted with disgust how thickly the asphyxiating smog hung over the city below. It entered his head that there was a lack of oxygen down there that clouded peoples' thinking. It was a relief to finally drive up the steep approach to their apartment, and know that H.A. was likely home already. He whistled as he parked his car and raced up the stairs, two at a time. There she was, working at the kitchen table.

"Good God," he exclaimed. "You look snowed under. You really must plan things better. No written work on Fridays, just oral stuff."

"Now why didn't I think of that before?" she laughed.

"Because you're too diligent, Miss Du Toit," he replied. "You think too much of those little minds waiting for you to enlighten them. You must think of other things, like me. How about enlightening me?"

"Okay, I'll think of nothing but you until Monday morning," she said, pushing her work aside and pulling his face down to hers.

"Mm, now that sounds like my kind of weekend," he murmured, "I definitely like the sound of that."

Helen smiled at him. "We don't have anything planned do we?"

"Unfortunately, Dave Marais has plans for us. He's got some great idea about solving the country's problems," he replied.

"What! Don't tell me he's emigrating? I still want to fix him up on a date with Mary Atkinson," she teased.

"God no, he wouldn't emigrate, H.A., anymore than we would."

"I'm not so sure actually. Sometimes I think there's no hope here. What do you think about him and Mary?"

"Well, judging by Dave's excitement earlier, I don't think he could stand any more excitement with Mary. He'd have a heart attack! We'll have to work on that one, but he wants us to go over to his place tonight and hear his plans."

"What about our weekend alone?"

"The sooner we get there, the sooner we can get back!"

He looked appreciatively at her long, slim body as she got up from

21

the table, and smiled as she blushed slightly. "Come here, my love," he said pulling her towards him. "God I wish we didn't have to go out. You don't know how much I want you right now."

"Oh, I think I do!" she retorted and moved away from him towards the bedroom. "How about skipping dinner?" she said over her shoulder.

It grew dark as they lay listening to the evening orchestra of crickets gradually replace the daytime chorus of Mynah birds. The Frangipani tree outside smelled sweetest at nighttime and the darkness was a gentle, safe haven from that other world. It was hard to rouse themselves and return to it.

Dave Marais lived around the corner from them, and they walked to his apartment. Like their own, his was the top floor of an old home that had been converted into apartments, leaving just a faint reminder of the gracious lifestyle that once had existed. David bounded to the door as they rung the bell, saying, "Come in, come in. Helen, here sit on the sofa." He cleared a pile of books and returned them to the bookshelf in order to make room for her. "Are you happy with Dvorak, or would you like something else?" he asked, as he turned the stereo down.

"Actually, I'd like a beer," said Al, wandering into the kitchen and opening the fridge. "Mind if I help myself? Want anything H.A.?"

"I'm sorry Helen," said Dave, embarrassed, "I wasn't thinking. Can I get you something?'

"No thanks," she smiled, "and I love 'The New World Symphony.' Good choice."

"My fiancé is a model of tact, we're the yin and yang theory personified!" laughed Al, opening a Lion Lager and lazily slumping into a chair. "So, Marais, how are you going to cause this big cock-up that'll be our salvation?"

"Well it's pretty simple, as I told you earlier. All we need to do is defend these passbook cases."

"But...."

"No, hear me out Al. I know what you're going to say. We can't do it on our own, that's obvious. But we don't have to. There are many of us in Durban who feel the same way about this inhuman law, and I daresay there are many people in the rest of the country too. What I propose doing is getting a group of us attorneys together to defend cases free of charge - and maybe other people who are interested to help financially. With a bit of luck we could have a ground swell of sympathizers. I really believe there are more people than we imagine who would like to see some sanity and humanity in South Africa. Nobody knows how to go about it without being banned or imprisoned. But this would be within the law. Not only that, with this new ruling handed down by the Supreme Court, we stand an even better chance of fouling up the courts."

"What's the new ruling?" asked Helena.

"Oh, it states that blacks now only have to produce their passbooks within a reasonable amount of time when asked to do so. In other words, they don't have to carry them on their person at all times," replied Dave. "Imagine how we can make a meal of that in court. It's going to the Appeal Court and is likely to be overthrown, but we can get in now before that and defend any person who has fallen foul of this abominable law."

"And then what?" inquired Helen. Al was staring fixedly at his friend all the while, nodding his head every now and again.

"Then it's a question of manpower. Last year, nearly one hundred and thirty-three thousand blacks, almost one third of the prison population, were arrested for failing to produce passbooks on demand. Each case takes about three minutes, so how much time do you figure is spent on them?"

"I don't teach Arithmetic I'm afraid, just History. But I would say three hundred and ninety-nine thousand minutes," laughed Helen.

"Exactly. Now if we can establish legal groups throughout the country to defend them, we could take about thirty minutes per case. Can you work that out?"

"Jeez, you should've told us to bring calculators," complained Al good-naturedly.

David had no time for levity. "To be brief, it would take ten times

23

as long, which works out to one hundred and eighty-eight thousand, five hundred *hours* of the court's time."

"I see where you're heading," said Al thoughtfully. "The existing court system couldn't cope with the extra time."

"Wouldn't the government just establish new courts?" Helen asked.

"Highly unlikely H.A. They don't have enough qualified staff for the existing ones."

"So what do you see happening then, David?" asked Helen.

"This is what I think. The government will have to ensure that fewer arrests are made. If they do that, we have an excellent case against them. If the law is not being properly enforced, then there's no need for the law. Simple as that! That's what we're aiming for ultimately, the repeal of the passbook laws. But before we can do that, our immediate object should be to provide adequate defense for all those desiring it."

Helen clasped her hands behind her head and frowned. "Don't you think the government would take away the power of the courts if that were to happen? I'd think they'd make it an automatic prison sentence, totally in the hands of the police."

"I thought about that, and it's a possibility. I don't think they'd risk it though. The outcry here and abroad would isolate them even more."

A heavy silence fell over the room as they all brooded on possible flaws in the argument. Helen was suddenly filled with foreboding that nothing in her life would ever be the same again. She sensed that they were jumping into very deep, dangerous water and she longed to be able to stop time, put it on rewind, and go off on a different track. She looked away and closed her eyes, but in her mind she saw a shark-infested ocean with a few helpless people on a sinking life raft. She froze as Al slammed down his beer can and said, "I reckon it might just work. What do you think H.A.?"

She grimaced. "It terrifies me. But," she shrugged and frowned again, "if we're not breaking the law, then, well... .I suppose ...."

That was all it needed for David to leap up and hug them both. "I know I said that we couldn't do it alone, but truthfully Al, I knew I couldn't do it without you. I have ideas, but you're the one who makes things happen."

"Let's get to it then!" Al urged. "H.A., can you get busy drafting a letter? You're good at that. Dave and I can compile a list of possible volunteers."

"Here, Helen," said David, offering her his notes, "you might want to look through these for ideas."

She sat cross-legged on the floor, perusing the file and chewing the end of a pencil. After a while she got up to turn over the record and stood staring at the city lights below. Al looked up at his fiancée and momentarily cursed, knowing in that instant how their lives were going to be pulled apart. She looked so beautiful standing there, deep in thought. At last he said gently, "How're you doing, H.A.?"

She turned to smile at him and they stared searchingly at one another a long time. She felt a stirring, remembering the pleasure of an hour ago and resented having to share him with this cause. She knew how much energy he threw into all he did, and she jealously wanted it all for herself.

He raised his eyebrows. "Are you having second thoughts my love? You look worried."

Scratching her forehead, she shook her head. "Yes and no. I just wish we could forget about all this stuff sometimes and live our lives, minding our own business. I suppose it's selfish really, but nothing we can do will ever change anything, and we could all get hurt in the process."

Dave excused himself and tactfully slipped out of the room. Al watched him leave and then put his arms around Helen. "H.A. I will never ask you to do anything you don't agree with. Likewise, I hope you would never expect me to do something against my principles."

"You know I wouldn't Al."

"So if you don't want to be part of this, that's fine. But you see, it's true what they say, that the easiest way for evil to flourish is if good people do nothing."

"I know, I agree with you. It's just that I also know that trouble will be walking right beside you. The police will find a way, any way, of stopping your efforts. I couldn't bear it if anything happened to you."

"It's all within the law. I'm not going to do anything dangerous, so nothing is going to happen to me. With all due respect to your father, the police are a bunch of idiots with lots of brute force but not too much brain. Dave and I won't break the law, my love. We'll be safe, I promise." He kissed the top of her head and then lifted her chin so that he could look in her eyes. "Hey, I know what's good for me and the lucky thing is that it's good for you too." He kissed her and pressed her tightly to him, "The most important thing in my life is you, always. But I can't ignore what's going on around me."

"I know that, and it's part of what I love about you."

"May I ask what the other part is?"

She smiled. "Okay, I'm back with the program. I'm sorry, I'm just not as brave as you are."

"H.A. I love everything about you and I need your voice of reason and caution. I can't imagine life without you."

"I hope you won't have to, I'm planning on being here to stay and I love you too. I need you in my life to be happy. So… I suppose, let's get back to the task in hand."

"Do you think Dave has locked himself in the toilet or something? Let me go and find him. He's probably too embarrassed to come back," Al laughed.

Helen was deep in thought when they returned and she looked up to say, "I'm ready to put pen to paper now. The way I see it, we're doing this not only for the blacks who are detained, but also for all of us, and for children as yet unborn in South Africa. We have to appeal to people's compassion and keep party politics out of it. We must present it as professional people performing their duty, not a political protest."

"Well said. Best not be quite as blunt as Dave and say we're screwing the system!" laughed Al.

By early morning they'd produced a list of names and a satisfactory draft proposal and on Monday, thirty-nine attorneys in Durban received this letter.

354 Smith Street,
Suite 20
Durban
11 October 1973

Dear Colleague,

As attorneys it is our duty to apply the law as we find it, whether we approve or not. It is for politicians to change the law. However it is also our duty to ensure that the law is applied with all due process, namely a fair trial.

Many laws, that remove their civil liberties, humiliate the black people of South Africa. We speak in particular of the law that requires blacks to possess passbooks in order to live and work in cities. The same law generally prevents a wife and children from living with their husband and father, as they are expected to remain in a rural area. Yet South Africans of other races are free to work and live where they choose.

We are establishing a Legal Group to offer advice and services, free of charge, to any person who has fallen foul of this abominable law. Members of the group will take it in turns to appear in court and defend accused persons, affording them a fair trial. We anticipate that the time taken in each case will increase from approximately three to thirty minutes, or longer if needs be.

We would like to be in court by the first of November. This is important, given the new ruling by the Supreme Court, which requires Blacks to produce a passbook within a reasonable amount of time, rather than carrying it on their person at all times. This ruling will soon go before the

Appeal Court, and we wish to be operating before that happens.

We invite you to join us as a founder member of the Legal Group. Although there will be no monetary reward, we believe that this is an issue of conscience. Justice will be its own reward. We hope to hear from you soon.

Sincerely,
Alan Griffin and David Marais
Tel: 031 263-310

Chapter 3

Johannesburg is a thriving city whose streets are underlined with gold. It is the second biggest city in Africa, where wealth and poverty live side by side.

In their elegant home in the Northern suburbs of this city of gold, Mr. and Mrs. Griffin were entertaining guests. The dining room in which they sat was large and impressive, with high ceilings, mahogany furniture and satin drapes. The formal effect was softened by candlelight that glimmered on the crystal and silver place settings. Despite the dignity of the room, there was warmth and easy conversation around the table. The Griffin's parties had a fine reputation.

The Vichyssoise had been a great success, and as Hilda Griffin rang the bell for her maid to clear for the second course, she attracted all attention with her remarks about her son's fiancé. "She's a pretty girl, but very quiet. I think, quite frankly, she's out of her depth. Never says a word, my dear. I don't understand Alan. Thank you, Dora that was excellent. You can bring in the roast lamb now."

"But my dear, it must be awfully uncomfortable for her if Afrikaans is her home language. Perhaps she doesn't understand everything you say," suggested Mavis Atherton-Jones, one of the guests.

"Well I hope Alan has the sense to speak only English to her. What good is a bastard language like that to anyone? Heaven forbid that my grandchildren should speak Afrikaans! I don't understand a word of it and I refuse to learn now. Quite honestly, I'd rather learn Zulu. It would be far more useful and Dora would appreciate it," was the offended mother's reply. "I don't understand where we went wrong," she continued. "We gave our son the best of everything and now he chooses to marry a policeman's daughter. His future was so bright, but what support can a wife like that give him? She'll be a hindrance to his career."

"Hilda my dear, the more you talk like that, the more you drive them together," reprimanded William Griffin sharply, as he poured more wine for the guests. "For some reason the young feel obliged to do everything differently. I know it's hard to bite your tongue, but it would be best."

"I quite agree with you, William," replied Bob Newton, an old school friend. "I wouldn't worry about it one bit if I were you. Perhaps when he sees no parental reaction, he'll come to his senses and drop the affair. Let him sow his wild oats!"

****

Four hundred miles away in Durban, Captain Fanus Du Toit and his wife Engela sat in their modest kitchen, drinking coffee and eating rusks before going to bed. The cuckoo clock next to the door had just struck nine and Wagter, the dog, barked angrily. It was time for him to go into the backyard and let the neighborhood know that he was on guard. The Captain opened the door and pushed the dog outside. "The trouble started when we first moved to Durban with all these damned English Liberals around," he grumbled as he poured more coffee. "Our daughter was no problem until then."

"No, my darling. When she was at school there was no problem because all her friends were Afrikaans," said Engela. As always, her voice was gentle.

"You're right about that. It was university with all those students who don't know what they're talking about. They think they know everything, when in fact they don't know their arses from their elbows! We should have sent her to Pretoria, but no, you wanted your daughter close to home. And now look; she doesn't even live here anymore. She doesn't even speak Afrikaans, except to us. She never sees any of her old friends, just the bloody fool Griffin and this Mary Atkinson. I don't think that girl can speak one word of Afrikaans."

"But Fanie, it's her life and she's getting married. We can't hold onto her forever," protested his wife.

"Engela, I don't like our future son-in-law, and that's that. It's a great sorrow to me that our only child has chosen to marry an Englishman, and worse still, one who will land himself in trouble. He's irresponsible. I'm telling you, half his friends are communists and the other half are black."

"Well you must talk to him Fanie," she replied. "If he loves our daughter, he'll respect what you say."

"The only thing that bastard would respect is my boot in his backside. I can't talk to him, I've tried, but you can't tell him anything. He scorns the Security Police. He has no idea that we risk our lives to save his skin. I don't know what we can do. Why couldn't she marry a good Afrikaans boy who would've called her Helena Anna as she was baptized, and not Helen or H.A.?" he fumed.

"A name doesn't matter Fanie. We must be grateful that she's happy and accept God's will," replied Engela. "He works in mysterious ways that we don't always understand. We've been happy together and we mustn't stand in her way of finding happiness, even if we don't like the boy."

"But this is different. We've been happy because we've worked hard together for honorable things. Here you've made a good Christian home to educate our daughter, and I've worked a thankless job in the police force."

"You can't say it's thankless Fanie. Look at your position now, you're Captain of the Security Police in Durban," corrected Engela proudly.

"Yes, you're right, but I get no thanks from the likes of Alan Griffin. I wish sometimes I could tell everybody about the things we're uncovering, things that threaten the safety of South Africa. People wouldn't believe it."

They both fell silent, lost in their own thoughts, nursing their anxieties and disappointments.

****

Mrs. Anna Gumede gently lowered a bucket of water, which she had been carrying on her head, and rubbed her back wearily. She watched her sister-in-law light a paraffin stove to cook their evening meal and felt a glow of gratitude. These relatives had looked after her since that day, long ago, when her husband had died in a mining accident in Johannesburg. Johannesburg, eGoli, City of Gold. It had brought them no riches, only sorrow.

She remembered the white farmer coming to give her news of her husband's accident. Everybody had known there was trouble when they saw him arrive in the village. Simon, her only child, was waist-high then and too small to understand that his father would never return. He didn't remember much about his father, but he always wanted to hear stories about the man. Now the boy was as tall as his father had been, and he was working in Durban. She had pleaded with him not to go to Johannesburg when the time had come to look for a job. "It's a bad place," she had said. "It's dangerous and you will be too far from home. Durban is only five hours on the bus. Johannesburg is two days. My child, please don't go there."

She proudly contributed all the money that Simon sent each month to buy food for their extended family. She longed to see her child again but contented herself with his letters that came each month, describing his new life. He had found a good friend called Philemon, who had helped him find a job and a place to stay. She enjoyed the satisfaction of knowing that her family valued her son too, and smiled when her sister-in-law sometimes said, "That boy, I think he will do good things. One day, all Zulus will be proud of Simon Gumede."

"Yes," Anna thought, "but I will be proudest of all."

Chapter 4

Simon Gumede felt very pleased with life. Since his arrival in Durban four months ago, his friend Philemon had helped him find two jobs and a place to stay. During the day he worked at Frazer's Moving and Storage Company in the city, where he was a packer. Philemon worked there too and had recently been promoted to boss-boy. They were always very busy packing up white people's furniture into big boxes and sending them to other countries. At night, Simon worked on the Kwa Mashu Committee with his friend. He was very happy and thankful for his good fortune.

He had come to Durban without a job. The only white people he had known were the children, long ago, on the farm. They had played together before the white kids went to boarding school, and then he'd never seen them again. Their father had come to the kraal once when Simon's father had died, and he remembered how all his adult relatives had respectfully looked away from the farmer, as if he were a great chief. He expected nothing from white people except employment, and would have been content to live all his days just a nameless face on a crowded bus, traveling to work, but for his humiliation by the police. He felt a deep resentment that was the only education he needed to prepare him for his new life in the city.

He sat now in Kwa Mashu Township with three other members of the committee, in the back room of Mama Gloria's eating-house. The smoke from the kerosene lamp and cheap cigarettes was trapped by poor ventilation, as the window was nothing more than a small hole in the wall, covered with sacking to keep out the night air. The room was dark and hazy, but its back exit was well known and easily located, providing a quick escape in the event of a police raid. Mama Gloria's beer was the best in Kwa Mashu, but her shebeen was also illegal. Only whites were allowed to brew or sell beer, but Mama Gloria was a proud Zulu, brewing beer the way her ancestors had always done before her, and a few recent laws weren't a deterrent.

The committee sat on wooden boxes around a rickety, wooden table. All of them, except one, had a tin full of beer in front of them. The exception was the secretary, Reverend Timothy Mkize. Philemon Dlamini was the chairman and he addressed the meeting. "Can we agree then, in view of the recent ruling of the Supreme Court, to arrange a meeting informing the people of Kwa Mashu about their rights? They no longer need to have their passbook with them at all times, but they must be able to produce it within a reasonable amount of time."

Rev. Mkize looked up from taking notes and slowly began speaking. "I feel it would be safer to wait and see whether the Supreme Court ruling will be changed by the Appeal Court. We have to be responsible in our leadership, not lead our people into confrontation with the police and the white authorities. If the ruling is overturned, we might not have time to inform our people and then they would be in big trouble, caused directly by us."

Simon, the newest and youngest member, was also not sure of his decision. He had been traumatized by his recent imprisonment and wished to avoid repeating that experience; yet he respected his mentor, Philemon, and had sworn to always follow his advice. "What would happen," he inquired, "if I threw my passbook away and said I'd lost it? What if we all did that?"

"Simon," said John Msomi, treasurer of the committee, a

misshapen man with a badly scarred face, "we mustn't seek confrontation with the police." He took a long drink of beer and belched quietly into his chest. "Their numbers are few, but their weapons are strong and the law will protect them." He drank again and continued, "Look at me. I didn't always look like this. No my friend. Hai! Once I walked straight like you, and my skin was smooth, but I argued with a white policeman who arrested my wife and child. Do you know what their crime was? They were living with me without passes. That policeman, you know what he did?" John took another long drink of beer and then banged the tin loudly on the table. "He arrested me too, for obstructing the police. That's not all. When I was in prison, he came to teach me a lesson because he said I was a cheeky kaffir. He handcuffed my wrists to my ankles, beat me all over with his baton, kicked me, and just to make sure, he stuck a broom handle up my arse. I had to go to hospital after that." He stared into his tin of beer and nodded his head as he reflected on this. "That's why I look like this."

Simon stared at him with horror. "Did you tell the doctor what he did to you?" he cried.

"I didn't have to tell him, he could see. But the policeman told him I'd fallen down some stairs and landed on a broom. That doctor was crying when he stitched me up and put me in a cast; I could just see a little through one eye, the other one was swollen shut. He wasn't allowed to give me anything for the pain, even when he stitched me. The policeman stood and watched all the time." He paused as he drank the last of his beer and then added deliberately, "Yes, that policeman taught me a very big lesson: that they are cruel bastards and I hate them. That's what I learned Simon, but I also learned to respect their power." He stared mournfully at his empty tin.

A heavy silence fell upon the room, broken only by the muffled shouts and drunken laughter coming from the crowded eating-house. Simon was confused. In the Mission School where he had studied until Standard Six, he had learned that good deeds were rewarded and bad ones punished. Now it seemed that good people got into terrible trouble, while those who lied and were bad, got into no trouble at all. He told this to Reverend Mkize.

"Well, you see Simon," the Reverend said sadly, "when the white man first came here, he had the Bible and we had the land. He gave us the Bible and then he took our land. Now he has to find reasons to justify his greed, so he says that God wanted us to be separate. He says black people are the descendants of Hamm, and we must be the hewers of wood and carriers of water. He says it's there in the Bible. It's a funny thing my friends," he looked around at all of them, "I remember that great man, Archbishop Tutu, saying that religion is like a knife. It's neither a good thing nor a bad thing. It depends what you use it for. I can give you a knife and you can use it to cut bread and feed people. I can also give you a knife and you can use it to kill a man."

Philemon nodded. "I agree with you Father Mkize, we must be responsible and use the knife to cut bread. I hear what you say too, John, the police are too powerful for us to stand against them. But we have the opportunity to make a stand without breaking the law. We must grab the opportunity while we have it. If the ruling is overturned, we'll hold another meeting and tell everybody. It's not a big problem. "

"But what will happen to people who don't come to the second meeting?" asked Simon anxiously. "They'll be caught without their passbooks."

"Yes," agreed Philemon, "they will. And they'll have to go to prison. But that's nothing new and the news will spread fast. It always does. I believe we should grab the opportunity and show our opposition to this law while we can. Once an American president said that the only thing to fear is fear itself." He looked solemnly at his committee. "He was also a great man, called Franklin Roosevelt, and he helped his allies to win a war. We're fighting a war now. We cannot give in to fear." He paused and then added, "Gentlemen, can we take a vote? All those in favor of holding a meeting to inform Kwa Mashu residents of the Supreme Court ruling, raise your hand."

Four hands went up.

"The motion is carried," announced Philemon. "Thank you my friends."

Chapter 5

Captain Fanus Du Toit sat at his desk on the ground floor of Security headquarters. He was a large, solid man in khaki uniform, with dark hair cut closely around his head. He had a habit of resting his chin in the palm of his hand and drumming his nose with his fingers. Then his fingers would slide down his nose and tug at his neat mustache. His eyes were fixed on a point just above the door as he concentrated on the report being given him.

Seated opposite him was Sergeant Kobus Erasmus, a man of average height and build who was able to mingle successfully in crowds without being noticed. His eyes were heavy-lidded but darted rapidly as he spoke. "The self-appointed Kwa Mashu Committee met again tonight, sir," he began. "They've decided to hold a public meeting, informing all blacks in Kwa Mashu that it's no longer necessary to carry their reference books. We'll have to watch Philemon Dlamini more closely. I understand he's a first class speaker, and tonight, he so inflamed the feelings of the committee that one member, Simon Gumede, advocated an open breach of the law. John Msomi apparently calmed him down, but Dlamini's a bad influence."

"Who is this Simon Gumede?" asked the Captain.

"He's a cheeky kaffir that Dlamini met in prison," replied Erasmus.

"You are not to use the word kaffir!" snapped Captain Du Toit. "You're a policeman and you should know better than to use inflammatory language."

"I'm sorry, sir," responded Erasmus, looking at his shoes.

"But I agree with you, this Dlamini requires attention. Organize a tail. If there's evidence of subversion by him, we may well have to ban the public meeting." He gazed thoughtfully at the top of the Sergeant's head and then continued, "On the other hand, we could detain him in terms of the Terrorism Act. Meantime, keep me informed of all his activities."

"Right, sir," replied Erasmus. "There's another problem that's arisen. A group of young attorneys have formed a Legal Group, that's what they call themselves."

"Students?" asked the Captain.

"No, sir. Practicing attorneys. They have a scheme to cause havoc' in the courts defending all the passbook cases, free of charge."

"Shit! Who are the organizers?"

"There appear to be two ring leaders, sir, Alan Griffin and David Marais." Erasmus paused and watched his superior officer carefully. The latter did not react, so the sergeant continued. "They held a meeting at Marais' home tonight with all the volunteers who plan to help. Your daughter was present at the meeting, sir, as the guest of Griffin."

"Sergeant, I don't need you to play nursemaid to my daughter and I assure you I'm well aware of her associates." The Captain altered his gaze and stared at the sergeant, who shifted uneasily.

"I was merely reporting something I thought would be of interest to you," he responded. Erasmus found it offensive to think of an Afrikaans girl and an Englishman together.

"Sergeant, you are aware that my daughter is engaged to Griffin. Carry on with your report."

"That's it, sir, except that this Legal Group plans to begin operations on the first of November."

"Shit!" the Captain said again. "The news will spread on the bloody bush telegraph, and within a week every black in Durban will know about it. By November, there'll be hordes of them wanting to use its services. You can rest assured that the Legal Group will work within the law so we're going to have a difficult time stopping this. Keep an eye on Marais' apartment and office and get them bugged. I want to be kept fully informed. Does Griffin still live with Marais?"

"No, sir." Erasmus looked embarrassed. He cleared his throat nervously. "Shall I bug his apartment as well?"

"Do it at once," barked the Captain, getting up to open the door so that Erasmus could leave. "And you'd better infiltrate the Kwa Mashu Committee with an informer."

Erasmus smiled. "I've already done so, sir, and I'll have Griffin's apartment bugged within a day. I'll think you'll find it informative." He turned on his heel and walked quickly down the corridor.

Captain Du Toit closed the door and slowly returned to his desk, where he opened a folder and made notes of his meeting with Erasmus. When he finally switched off the light to return home, he thought with satisfaction that his devotion to duty helped keep South Africa sleeping soundly.

Chapter 6

The first of November was a humid day, with jacaranda trees and tibouchina bushes heavily in bloom, adding to the mauve haze that was already hanging lazily over the city. The rush hour traffic streamed along the main arteries as usual, racing to the heart of the business and industrial districts. But today there was also a stream of people jostling their way to the Durban Magistrate's Court. The bush telegraph had done its work well, and the public galleries were crammed with noisy spectators and journalists, wanting to see the Legal Group in action. There was a hum of chatter and laughter. Those who were unable to get a seat within, waited outside in the crush. In the cells there was also a sense of excitement and anticipation.

When five young attorneys finally entered the courtroom, the crowd cheered them wildly, as if they were gladiators entering the Roman Coliseum. Three others, Angus Reeve, Pat Moodley, and John Ngcobo, had joined Al and David. They looked in amazement at the courthouse filled to capacity, and smiled at each other as they seated themselves at the Bar. This was a series of tables arranged in front of the Magistrate's bench, where they were able to set out their books and documents in neat rows. They'd had numerous meetings during the previous weeks and needed no discussion now. Just as well, as it would have been impossible above the noise of the courtroom.

Al Griffin felt exhilarated, like a well-trained athlete before a big race. He looked at his colleagues who also appeared eager to get going, and felt complete confidence in all of them. He understood Dave like he understood himself; and Angus, with his fiery temperament inherited from a Scottish grandparent, was tenacious and formidable. Pat Moodley came from a family of attorneys in Verulum, Natal. Although as an Indian South African he was not required to carry a passbook, he had many other grievances against a system that denied him equal rights because of his skin color. This fired him with energy that, coupled with his sharp intelligence, made him an asset to the group.

John Ngcobo had perseverance to achieve the impossible. It is not easy for a black man to educate himself in South Africa. John had gone to a small farm school where his brightness and determination had helped him win the notice of a local teacher and the farmer's wife. They had helped and encouraged him to complete his schooling, even compensating his parents who had wanted him to stop when he was twelve to look after the goats. He had then done his legal training at Fort Hare, while working at any job he could get in his spare time. Resentfully he carried his passbook as required, but looked for ways to change the system. He felt a responsibility to his fellow black South Africans to be a spokesperson for them.

It had been a disappointing response to their letter, but Al and Dave considered that it was fear, rather than apathy, that had deterred many people. Today was just the beginning step in a long journey. Any apprehension they felt was dispelled as the robed magistrate entered the courtroom through a door behind the Bench, like an emperor entering the Coliseum. A policeman yelled, "Rise in court," as the magistrate bowed and took his seat. There was still a hum of noise, however, which was unacceptable.

"If there is not complete silence in this court, I will have it cleared," the magistrate announced sternly and the policeman made a move towards the gallery. The room immediately became silent.

The prosecutor, who was sitting at the far end of the Bar, rose and called the first case. A prisoner dressed in shabby overalls, was led into the dock from a side door. He cringed nervously until he caught sight of the five attorneys. His face brightened as a light of hope came into his eyes.

"Amos Mdluli," droned the prosecutor, "you are charged with the crime that on or about the thirty-first of October, 1973, and in the city of Durban, you did wrongfully and unlawfully fail to produce your passbook to a police officer on demand. Do you plead guilty or not guilty?"

"My boss," the prisoner said to the magistrate, "I want an attorney to defend my case."

"Have you engaged the services of an attorney?"

"No, my boss."

Rising to his feet, Alan Griffin spoke loudly and clearly. "Your Worship, should the accused so require, I am prepared to represent him."

"Do you want this man to be your attorney?" the magistrate inquired of the prisoner.

"Yes, my boss."

"In that case, Your Worship," responded Alan, "I request that the trial in this matter be adjourned until tomorrow, as I wish to take instruction from my client and prepare his defense."

"Would you like to take instruction now, Mr. Griffin?" asked the magistrate. "We can adjourn the case for half an hour."

"No thank you, Your Worship," replied Alan. "I want to be available to any other prisoners who might call upon my services. I'll make arrangements to visit the accused this afternoon when he's been returned to prison."

"Then this case stands adjourned until nine o'clock tomorrow morning," ordered the magistrate. "The accused is to remain in custody."

The next case was duly called and David Marais arose to offer his services. The Legal Group continued to take turns at this for two hours, when the last of the passbook cases had been called. Each one of the accused now had an attorney.

The Legal Group spent the rest of the day interviewing their new clients at the Durban Central Prison. Initially the prison officials had refused to allow the interviews, but they'd relented when threatened with a court order. The surly, armed guards stood watch furiously, as the mammoth task of taking statements from the prisoners was carried out. It was evening by the time the attorneys had finished and wearily left the prison. They were hopeful that the next day would start to show results.

There was still a knot in Alan's stomach as he returned pensively to his office. He needed to clear his desk of today's mail, and compose his thoughts about tomorrow's defense. In such unchartered territory he felt like Columbus, believing in his quest, yet still nervous he might fall off the edge of the world at any moment. Suddenly he was aware of a large black man, leaning against the locked door to his office. It was late and the staff had already gone home. Al approached cautiously.

"Good evening, Mr. Griffin," the man said, straightening up and putting out his hand in a courteous gesture. "My name is Philemon Dlamini. I'd like to talk to you about your work with the passbook cases."

"Good evening, Mr. Dlamini," said Alan, standing aside and holding the door open for the other man. "Come into my office. We can talk there." He closed the door and locked it, before leading Philemon inside. Sinking into a chair, he gestured at another opposite him and said gently, "Please sit down. Have you been caught without a passbook?"

Philemon looked intently at Alan, considering both the man and what he should say. "I've been caught many times on that account, but it's not a personal matter that I wish to speak about." He paused thoughtfully. "I am the chairman of an unofficial body called the Kwa Mashu Committee, and I speak on their behalf. We deal with human rights and try to offer advice to the people of Kwa Mashu. We have very few funds, but we would like to retain your services for one special occasion."

"What's that?" asked Al.

"Tomorrow evening we are holding a public meeting at the sports stadium in Kwa Mashu, to inform people of their rights with regard to passbooks and the recent Supreme Court ruling. I'm sure you know all about that, Mr. Griffin," smiled Philemon.

Alan nodded his head and smiled.

Philemon continued. "We're aware of how much you are already doing for us and we really appreciate it, but we would like to ask one more thing. Please will you come to this meeting tomorrow night and explain to the people their exact legal rights?"

"Much as I would like to, I can't do that Philemon. Unfortunately I have to have the prior permission of the Natal Law Society, and there isn't sufficient time to get that. What I can do perhaps, is sit on the platform with you and your committee. You can tell me what you plan to say and I'll tell you if your interpretation of the law is correct. Of course, this is providing I'm able to get a permit to enter Kwa Mashu tomorrow." He laughed at the irony as they both shook their heads scornfully.

"It's not even a free country for you, Mr. Griffin!"

"Please, call me Alan. It sounds like we're on the same wavelength. If I can do this for you, it'll be as a member of the Legal Group, so there'll be no charge. What you can do for us is announce that any person arrested for not producing a passbook can use our services. We plan to have at least two members of the Legal Group on duty every day in court."

"We're very grateful, Alan. This is a lot of extra work for you." He cleared his throat and carefully explained what he planned to say the following night. Al listened intently with his hands clasped behind his neck. As Philemon finished, the attorney leaned forward, placing his elbows on the desk.

"Your understanding of the law and the recent Supreme Court ruling appear to be sound, Philemon. I don't think it can be said that you are inciting people to disobey the law, which would be considered subversive. No, I think that's all very sound and informative." He smiled, adding, "You're a very courageous man. I'd be honored to join you tomorrow night."

"Thank you very much. There'll be thousands of people at the meeting tomorrow. It's good that they'll be able to see you, hopefully, and know that there are white people who will fight for them too."

When the two men parted, deeply impressed with each other, they shook hands like lifelong friends. Two tiny boats, lost in the ocean, had thrown out ropes and linked together, combining forces against the frightening current. They were rowing together in the same direction.

As he arrived home and opened the door of their apartment, Alan heard the phone ringing. He rushed to answer and immediately felt his patience snap. Closing his eyes, he held the receiver six inches from his ear and listened. Helen came around the corner and looked quizzically at him as he said, "I'm afraid that's out of the question. I'm committed to defending my clients and I wouldn't dream of dropping the whole thing now."

He paused, rolled his eyes and mouthed at Helen, "My father!" She could hear a torrent of angry words on the other end of the line before her fiancé said crisply, "That's where you're wrong. It doesn't matter to me whether they're paying or not, they're still my clients. The object of my career is to see justice done, not just to make money!"

There was a pause as he listened.

"I appreciate your concern Dad, but that's not my idea of success at all. Sorry to disappoint you, but rest assured I'll never be successful by your standards." More words came from the other end before the conversation ended abruptly.

"Oh dear, what's that all about?" asked Helen.

"He's just read the paper and phoned to say I'm ruining my career. I need to quit this ridiculous nonsense immediately! Unbelievable! Does he think I'm still ten years old and that I need him to tell me what's right and wrong?"

"Don't get so irritable, he cares about you, Al. It's just unfortunate that he sees things differently. It's the same with my Dad."

"It's damn unfortunate, and damn different. Have they no conscience? Who has the correct idea here about what's right and wrong?" he asked with exasperation.

"Just ignore it, maybe it'll go away," she said.

"I don't know how you can always just shrug off stuff like that, H.A."

"There are some things that you can't change, so I don't see the point in hitting your head against a wall. Maybe growing up with my Dad taught me just to tune out and get on with my life the way I want it to be."

Al scowled and said, "I can't do that. It's not just something between them and us. It's much bigger than that."

"I know it is, but you're not going to change them by fighting with them. Anyway, tell me what happened today. I wanted to be there so badly."

She listened to his account of the crammed court and the day's proceedings, the interviews with the prisoners, and finally the meeting with Philemon.

"Won't you need a permit to go into Kwa Mashu?" she inquired.

"Sure I do, but John Ngcobo has a friend at Bantu Affairs who'll be able to arrange it. It's not a problem," he replied.

"Remember you promised not to go breaking the law, Alan Griffin. It won't help our cause."

"I won't my love, don't worry," he said, putting his arms around her gently. "The worst thing about all this is the time spent away from you."

"I know. I don't like it either," she said, reaching up to kiss him. "I'll go and visit my parents tomorrow night. That'll save you a visit. I know how you hate it."

"That sounds bad. I don't think your parents like me too much, H.A. Not quite what they had in mind for you, my love. Their ideas are about as narrow-minded as my folks'!"

"They're all afraid of anything different. I know how you feel about your Dad, Al, I don't mean to sound unsympathetic. I've reached a point where I dread talking to mine too. You know how he is - he still sees me as a little girl and can't accept that I've changed. He won't even begin to try and discuss anything because he's so used to giving orders. That's all he's done all his life. He makes me feel such a creep for being different. My Mom doesn't, but you know he rules her so she's never going to side with me against him about anything. I think they share a brain." Then she added, "If only they could see that there's plenty to go around for everybody in this country - it just needs to be shared evenly - but they never will."

They didn't talk much more after that. They both felt exhausted and welcomed the comfort of sleep and oblivion when at last it came.

Chapter 7

Al was in his office early the next morning, clearing his desk and leaving messages for his secretary on a Dictaphone. His partners had agreed that he should spend as much time as possible on the passbook cases, but he felt obligations to them and his other clients to carry a share of the normal workload. He worked through breakfast, only grabbing a cup of coffee before rushing off to join other members of the Legal Group for the day's battle in court.

He had to fight his way through crowds again, which seemed even larger than the previous day. Although it was early, the sun beat down with a fierce heat that foretold a scorching day. Summer had arrived with all its intensity except for those fortunate few with air conditioners. Al wiped his brow as he made his way into the courtroom to join his colleagues at the Bar. He looked around as he settled himself, and saw the smiling face of his new friend, Philemon, seated in the public gallery. They both nodded their heads in acknowledgement as Al leaned back in his chair to regain his breath.

At nine o' clock, the Magistrate arrived and took his place on the Bench. He had no need to silence the court, as an immediate hush of anticipation accompanied his arrival. The only sound was the order,

"Rise in court."

The first case was one of Alan's clients. Standing up he announced, "I appear for the accused, Your Worship. He pleads not guilty to the charge." He cleared his throat and sat down again.

The Prosecutor arose and looked impatiently at Al, saying, "In that case, I call as witness for the State, Constable Nyoka."

The court was crowded with policemen and Al realized that the Prosecutor had done his homework well, ensuring that all his witnesses were present. No accused would be freed on a technicality. A black policeman entered the witness box, where the oath was administered.

"What is your name and occupation?" asked the Prosecutor.

"I am a Bantu Constable, Elias Nyoka, stationed at the Point Police Station, Durban."

"Have you ever seen the accused before?" asked the Prosecutor, indicating the prisoner in the dock.

"Yes," replied the Constable, consulting a small notebook. "On Wednesday night, the thirty-first of October, 1973, at approximately nine-thirty, I saw the accused walking along Point Road in a northerly direction."

"What, if anything, did you do then?"

"I approached the accused and asked him for his passbook. He told me he did not have it, and so I searched him to confirm this. Then I arrested him."

"I have no further questions, Your Worship," said the Prosecutor, resuming his seat.

"Do you have any questions, Mr. Griffin?" asked the Magistrate, looking down at Alan from the Bench.

"Yes, thank you, Your Worship." Al stared thoughtfully at the witness. "Constable, when you first saw the accused, did he appear to be acting in a suspicious way at all?"

"No."

"He wasn't behaving in a suspicious manner. Then why did you decide to stop him, question him and make him suffer the indignity of being searched?"

"Mr. Griffin," snapped the Magistrate, "there is nothing in the evidence to suggest that the search was undignified."

"If Your Worship considers that it is dignified for a person going about his lawful purpose to be stopped and searched, then I withdraw the word undignified," said Alan, bowing his head. Turning to the Constable he continued, "Now please tell us why you stopped the accused to question and search him?"

"Because, due to the large number of thefts in this area, we have instructions to check the passbooks of all Bantu there after dark."

"Did you have any reason to suspect the accused of being a thief, Constable?"

"No."

"Now, Constable, when you use the word Bantu, does this mean a black person, an African?"

"Yes."

"Why don't you check the identity documents of whites?"

The constable looked scornfully at Alan and shook his head. He laughed and replied, "Because white people don't have to carry them."

"Let's move to another point," Al responded quickly. "Did you ask the accused where his passbook was?"

"Yes, he said he had left it at home."

"Did you give him time to collect it and show it to you?"

"No, of course not."

"Of course not," repeated Al. "I have no further questions," he said, sitting down and folding his arms.

"Any further witnesses?" the Magistrate asked the Prosecutor.

"No, Your Worship. That concludes the case for the State."

Turning to Alan, the Magistrate asked, "Do you have any witnesses you wish to call, Mr. Griffin?"

"Only one, Your Worship. I wish to call the accused."

As Constable Nyoka stepped down, the accused nervously left the dock to take the witness stand and give his evidence. After the oath had been administered, Alan asked him, "Do you have a passbook?"

"Yes, but I was in a hurry and left it at home."

"Where is your home?"

"In Kwa Mashu."

"And if necessary, could you produce your passbook?"

"Yes, I could."

"How long would it take you?"

"It depends on the buses. Sometimes they are full and then we must wait for another bus."

"So, if you did not have to wait too long, how quickly could you get your passbook and return to the police station in Point Road?"

"Maybe one hour."

"And if you had to wait for another bus?"

"Maybe two hours."

"No further questions," said Al, sitting down again.

"No questions," said the Prosecutor, as the Magistrate looked at him inquiringly.

"Is that the case for the defense, Mr. Griffin?" The Magistrate was incredulous.

"Yes, Your Worship," replied Alan.

The Magistrate raised his eyebrows and then frowned. He nodded at the Prosecutor, "Do you wish to address the court?"

"No, Your Worship, except to ask that the accused be found guilty as charged."

"Do you wish to address the court, Mr. Griffin?"

"Yes please, Your Worship," said Alan, rising and moving out into front of the court. "In the recent Supreme Court case of Zikilali versus the Minister of Police, the court decided that a Bantu who fails to produce his passbook on demand, is guilty of an offense. That is not disputed in the present case. What is disputed is the meaning of the words 'on demand.'

"In Zikilali's case, the Judge ruled that there was no offense committed provided that the person whose passbook was demanded, could produce it without involving the police in any traveling, and within a reasonable amount of time." He paused significantly. " That being the law, Your Worship, as decided by the Supreme Court, I submit that the accused be found not guilty. My client was given no chance at all to produce his passbook."

All eyes turned to the Magistrate. He coughed nervously and cleared his throat. Then he took off his glasses and wiped them before putting them firmly back on his nose. It was for him to pronounce judgment. Nobody moved. He swallowed hard. "The court will adjourn until after tea," he said gruffly.

With one voice, the crowd groaned. The noise level rose instantly. Dave grinned at his friend. "You've got him worried, Al."

"Let him sweat over that," grunted John Ngcobo.

Al looked anxious. "The verdict must obviously be 'not guilty.' Why the hell does he need to have a cup of tea? He's probably checking the law or getting directions from the Minister of Police. Anything can happen if that's the case."

"He's probably just gone for a pee," said Pat Moodley. "He looked a bit distended!"

They all laughed nervously, but it didn't relieve the tension. So much hung in the balance. After a while, the Magistrate returned to the Bench and a deathly quiet fell over the courtroom. He adjusted his glasses once more, and then proceeded to deliver his short judgment.

"I am obviously bound to follow the decisions of the Supreme Court. That being so, I must agree with Mr. Griffin and find the accused not guilty. He is accordingly discharged."

The last words were lost in the roar of the crowd. The public galleries erupted and well-wishers swarmed over the Legal Group, thumping them on their backs and shouting congratulations. The time was nine-forty a.m. The police tried to quell the noise, but by this time the news had reached those waiting outside. The doors burst open, letting in a fiery furnace of heat and more hysteria. Realizing that only time would quiet the jubilation, the magistrate tried to shout above the noise, "Court will adjourn for a short while." He, too, was boisterously congratulated as he hastened to the safety of his office.

The pandemonium continued for another fifteen minutes before the Legal Group was able to corner the Prosecutor and find out his intentions. "I don't see that I have much option but to withdraw charges in the remaining passbook cases," he told them curtly. He glared at them, then turned abruptly on his heel and walked away.

"Oh baby!" exclaimed John Ngcobo, "what a clean sweep. I didn't think he'd give up so easily."

"I can't believe it! It was almost too easy," said Pat. "Dammit Al, I didn't even get a chance to say my piece." He punched him playfully on the arm.

"That was just the first battle, I'm afraid. They'll be getting more ammunition as we speak, you can be sure of that. We haven't won the war - yet!" Al cautioned. "But I need to tell you all something interesting."

Briefly, he told them of his meeting the previous evening with Philemon, and his promise to appear at the meeting that night, if possible. John Ngcobo smiled and said, "You won't believe this, but I already know about the meeting. That's how things work in Kwa Mashu. You tell five people, and five hundred know within the hour. But I didn't know about you being there, Al."

"I was hoping your friend at the Bantu Affairs Department could get me a permit, John," he said, "otherwise I won't be there."

"No problem. I'll get you one and we can go together. Obviously I don't need one."

"I'd like to come too," said Pat Moodley, "if that's okay with you."

"Great. It'll be a show of solidarity. You'd better check with your friend and see whether Pat needs a permit too. It's a bit complicated knowing just who's allowed to go where! But I think that Dave and Angus shouldn't come, because if there's any complication with our friends finding a white face in Kwa Mashu, it's better that it's only one white face, not three. The Legal Group can manage with four attorneys, but not two."

While waiting for further court proceedings, they quickly made arrangements to meet that night and formed a roster for the rest of the month, ensuring legal advice was available for anyone needing it. At last the Magistrate returned and silence once more was restored in the courtroom. For two hours, a monotonous line of prisoners was brought before the Bench and the Prosecutor formally withdrew the charges against each one.

Suddenly the edge was taken off the victory as a door opened and a group of security policemen silently entered the courtroom. The untrained eye might have considered them ordinary police, but everything in their sinister demeanor set off alarm bells in Al's head. He watched them silently making notes and survey the crowd malevolently. Grimacing, he caught Dave's eye. They nodded their heads knowingly. It was clear they were faced with a formidable opponent and the next battle line was already forming.

Chapter 8

There is a mesmerizing quality in the darkness of an African night. The lack of city lights make the countless stars seem brighter and closer, and night creatures loudly assert their ownership rights. As Al and Pat drove to meet John along the old North Coast Road, their headlights beamed occasionally on the endless hills of sugarcane as they twisted and turned, but nothing else was visible. They didn't speak as they listened to the only sounds: the quiet hum of their car and the choir of insects. Solitude enveloped them.

As arranged, John Ngcobo was waiting in his old Plymouth at the Kwa Mashu turnoff. He responded to Al's flicking lights by pulling slowly into the road leading to the township. The cars bounced as they hit some potholes, and dodged others, until they slowly entered the smoky township, bathed in half-light. A thick haze from coal stoves surrounded the endless rows of small houses that all looked the same, and the acrid air burnt everyone's eyes. Chinks of light were visible through cracks in doors, and periodically a dim streetlight stood like an apologetic sentry, throwing off a welcome dot of light. Al could sense dark, featureless forms in the night. Watching. Waiting. The calm beauty of the cane fields had gone and the night had become threatening. They passed a cluster of shanty homes built out of whatever the builder had been able to glean, and the dusty walls fluttered in the slight breeze as they went by.

"Pat," murmured Al hoarsely, "I had no idea it was like this. I'm stunned." He almost sobbed as he whispered, "What does life hold for these poor people? It's not just their passes, it's their lives."

"I know," said Pat softly. "It's an existence, not a life."

They drove past a small shop that sold Afro Cola and Kara Skin Cream. Signs showing happy faces using these products were displayed in windows protected by heavy, iron bars. It was impossible to know what else was for sale, as nothing more was visible despite the few extra streetlights around the store. Orange cigarette ends pulsed like S.O.S signals in the forbidding streets.

Al was relieved when they arrived at the stadium, full of life and noise. The entire grassy playing area was full of people chanting and dancing. Women's shrill voices could be heard ululating, and then came deep responses from the men. Drumbeats pounded from somewhere in the crowd, prompting wild shouts of "Amandla" and "Freedom." The light here, though still inadequate, was better than in the streets. It felt safer to Pat, although Al felt himself sweating nervously. He'd been unnoticed in his car, but now as he emerged, his white face was exposed to the hostile glare of those close enough to spot him. He felt panic rising as his heart started to pound, sounding louder to him than the drums. He had an urge to get back into his car and leave at once, forgetting all ideas of attending the meeting.

"Come on Al," urged John, sensing his colleague's reluctance. He put a reassuring arm on his shoulder and said, "Your car will be safe. The Committee has organized a guard. Nobody will touch it. Just stick close to me and keep moving."

Al reddened and was thankful that the dim light concealed his embarrassment. He was ashamed of his hesitation and quickly followed John and Pat into the stadium to find Philemon. This was not a difficult task as a platform had been erected in front of the soccer posts and the tall man stood on it, towering over everyone else. Hurricane lamps had been set up for extra light, playing grotesquely on the faces of those standing directly above them. The shadows distorted features and even Philemon's familiar face looked strangely eerie.

Al's uneasiness was dispelled when his new friend saw him and shouted warmly, "You made it! Come up here and meet everyone. Bring your friends with you." Philemon was in control here and Al was thankful, realizing how vulnerable he'd felt when the crowd had surrounded him. Now he had the protection of its leader.

Members of the Legal Group were quickly welcomed and introduced to the rest of the Kwa Mashu Committee, before they all took their seats to start the meeting. Al noted how easily Philemon was able to call order by simply standing with his arms raised. The crowd immediately began to quieten, and within minutes, without a word from Philemon, all the chanting and drumming stopped completely and there was absolute silence. Only then did he address them.

"Friends," Philemon began, "Before we proceed with our meeting tonight, I will ask our Secretary, Reverend Mkize, to open with a prayer for us."

The priest rose from his chair and stood next to Philemon. He spread his arms, as if embracing the crowd, and tilted his face up to the Heavens. "Oh God, Creator of all and Father of our Lord, Jesus Christ, look upon this meeting tonight with pity. See and hear our plight. Help us, as you helped the children of Moses when you divided the waters. Divide, too, the waters that hold us back and lead us into our Promised Land. Grant us justice, oh Lord. Grant us strength to overcome our burdens and faith to know that you will always be by our sides. This we ask in the name of your Son, our Lord and Savior, Jesus Christ. Amen."

"Amen," echoed solemnly around the stadium.

"Please join with me now in singing our African National Anthem, Nkosi Sikeleli Afrika, God Bless Africa."

Al felt a chill down his spine as he heard the perfect harmony of about one thousand voices fill the night. He looked at Philemon as they sang and saw tears in the big man's eyes. Singing with him at that moment, Al felt a unity with Africa that gave him clearer insight of what he wanted to achieve than he had ever had before.

The anthem ended and as Reverend Mkize sat down, Philemon addressed the crowd again. His booming voice rang out across the stadium. "Brothers and sisters, welcome and thank you for coming. I know it's not always easy to get here, but I'm glad you made it. Let me introduce you to our guests tonight, Mr. Alan Griffin, Mr. John Ngcobo and Mr. Pat Moodley. These gentlemen are all attorneys and members of the Legal Group that many of you know about already. Later I will tell you more about their work, but first I want to tell you about an exciting change in our lives.

"The government of South Africa says that we black people must live and develop separately from them, and they give this a name. They call it Apartheid."

Angry shouts erupted in the crowd, but stopped as Philemon continued to speak.

"Apartheid; what that means for you and me, my friends, is that we must have permission to live here in this paradise called Kwa Mashu. Then we can get a passbook to travel into Durban where we can work for white people, cleaning their houses and swimming pools, things like that, but making sure that we are back here in our paradise by ten o' clock. At night Durban must be white, unless we blacks have a night shift job, then we need to get permission again for that."

As shouting started again, Philemon raised his arms once more. "We blacks suffer together my friends and we learn bitter lessons, but we don't suffer alone. There are many good people from other races too, who fight with us for our civil rights. It's because of people like this that the Supreme Court has passed a new ruling about our passbooks. Listen carefully to me."

He paused to make sure that he had their attention. "You still need your passbooks. Please understand that. But this new ruling says that we no longer have to carry them with us!"

The response was deafening. Excited screams rose above the roar of approval and the spontaneous hand clapping. There were more shouts of "Freedom!" and clenched black fists raised in salute.

"Let me finish," commanded Philemon. "Listen! You must still keep your passbooks at home safely. If a policeman stops you now, and he demands to see your pass, he must give you time to go and fetch it and bring it to the police station. You must be able to do this within a reasonable amount of time, maybe two hours, and you will not be breaking the law."

"Hey, Philemon," shouted an angry voice from the crowd. "That's too much trouble. Why must I pay to come all the way back here for my passbook? It's easier just to take it with me."

"Yes," agreed another. "This is nothing exciting. What are you talking about?"

Philemon raised his arms again as more shouts erupted. "I know it's difficult for us, but I'm talking about making it difficult for the police too. You see, if we do this, we make more work for them and then maybe they'll decide to stop passbooks altogether. And especially because now we have these friends, the Legal Group, working to help us." He turned and smiled at the three men. "Let me explain what they are already doing.

"If someone was arrested for not having a passbook in the past, as you know, that person went to prison, or had to pay a fine. None of us could ever pay for an attorney. From now on, that has changed. There will always be two attorneys from the Legal Group present in the Magistrate's Court, who will defend us, free of charge."

The laughter and cheering were even louder than the shouting had been. "Yes," Philemon continued, "look at these men. They are good men. Already there have been many people freed because of them. If they can take the trouble to help us, then we must take the trouble to help ourselves. Do you agree?"

The approving roar gave him his answer. The volume was so great that the wooden platform vibrated.

"We have solidarity then," he beamed. "From tomorrow, we will all leave our passbooks at home. We know we'll be stopped, but now we know that we are allowed to come back here to fetch them. We know that if we have to go to court for this, we will have an attorney to defend us and set us free. It's not going to be easy, but eventually the police will leave us alone because it'll be too much trouble.

"We can't break our chains with violence, because the police have guns and they'll shoot us. But we can try to break our chains this way with peaceful protest, and the attorneys will be there to defend us." He turned and applauded the Legal Group. Then he addressed the crowd again, "Good luck my friends, and go safely. If you have questions, please feel free to come and speak to the committee."

The meeting ended with the crowd bursting into more song as they slowly returned to their homes with hopes of change. Philemon beamed at the three guests as he walked with them to their cars, which were safe where they'd left them. "Thank you for all your trouble. Nothing I say can express how much we appreciate it."

"Philemon," Al said, "Nothing I say can express my shame for what has been done to your people by mine." He shook his head and then, opening his car door, added, "We'll get this right together so that you can be free, and my conscience can be clear."

****

Simon helped the other members clear the platform and then decided to go back to the hostel without Philemon, who was very busy answering questions. The young man strolled pensively, dreading the prospect of another night in prison if he were stopped. He thought of his mother at home on the farm and how he longed to see her again, but he couldn't afford to visit her, and he didn't want to live there again. "The work I'm doing is important," he told himself, "I can't go back. That was the place of my youth."

His thoughts were interrupted by two strange men who appeared out of nowhere and started walking on either side of him. Simon's instinct was to run, but he was frozen with fear. One of them began to speak, calling him by his name.

"Simon, we greet you," he said, "we won't harm you. We just want to talk to you as we walk. I am Joe and this is my brother Sipu."

Sipu then began to speak. "We've been watching you and your friend Philemon. He's teaching you many things, but he is old, like our fathers and grandfathers. We mustn't think like them anymore Simon. We're young and we are the future of South Africa. We must change things."

"Do you want to wait all your life trying to make things happen peacefully? Then maybe one day your grandson will enjoy what you want now," asked Joe with a sneer.

"Don't answer yet, Simon," said Sipu. "Philemon is a good man, so are all our fathers and grandfathers. But they are afraid and unorganized and their ways don't work. We want change and we want it in our lifetimes."

"So what have you got that Philemon hasn't?" asked Simon, skeptically.

"The courage to use violence," Joe said quickly. " We want the white man to sweat fear. He has everything to lose; we have nothing. We are able to get weapons and build an army to fight here, in South Africa, in these white cities, not miles away on the borders. We want to blow up power stations and police stations, maybe some airports and oil refineries. The whites think they're safe in their big houses with burglar alarms, but it's not going to help them when we're organized. Not even with all their police and armies. It won't be enough just to sacrifice their white sons on the borders of South Africa, because they'll need to defend themselves here."

"We'll never have enough power to fight them. You're mad!" exclaimed Simon.

Joe laughed. "Oh, we will. They call it terrorism but we call it guerilla war. We are Freedom Fighters. They won't know where to find us; we'll be a faceless army in the night. We'll blow up targets and then disappear."

Sipu continued, "You'd be a good Freedom Fighter, Simon. You'd be trained, in another country, to use arms and ammunition with many others who feel the same way. Or maybe they'll send you to school and even university. Then you'll come back here ready to fight for our freedom."

"Who is going to do this? Who's 'they' that you talk about?" Simon asked warily.

"The Congress. Haven't you heard about it? The A.N.C. The government has banned it and sent some of our leaders to prison. But there are other leaders in exile and they work to change things from overseas. Think about it. Philemon is a toothless old dog with no bite. We'll contact you again." With that they slipped away into the darkness as silently and suddenly as they'd appeared.

Simon was stunned and thought for a moment he'd been dreaming. Then anger welled up inside him. "They're madmen," he thought, "Philemon is good and wise. What they say would just spill our blood, that's all. Where do they think we can get guns? They steal a few pistols and think they can defeat the South African Defense Force! I'll tell Philemon tomorrow."

Chapter 9

The third of November 1973 was a day that would remain ingrained in Philemon Dlamini's memory forever. He arrived home from the meeting just before midnight with his mind still racing, and sat on the edge of his bed going through the night's events. He checked his notes made in Alan Griffin's office and thought about his speech again, wondering if he had omitted anything. It was good to be back in the stillness of his small room, which was bare except for an old iron bed, a blanket, and his battered suitcase under the bed, containing all his worldly belongings. He was glad he didn't have to live in a dormitory. Lying back he closed his eyes, but sleep wouldn't come. He felt physically exhausted, but his mind would not rest with the responsibility of leadership weighing heavily on him. The threadbare curtain flapped softly in the breeze and he lay watching it, until eventually he dozed off.

Bang, bang, bang. He woke with a start and sat up abruptly. Bang, bang, bang. He heard it again and registered that it was someone at his door. He looked at his watch and saw that it was only four o' clock in the morning. Bang, bang, bang, the infernal noise continued. He swung out of bed and made for the door, grumbling, "I'm coming.

Stop all the noise."

"Open immediately. It's the police," a voice shouted back at him. Philemon wasn't alarmed by this news. A police raid was a frequent occurrence during the night, as they searched the township for people without permits. He opened the door cautiously to verify that it was the police, and as he did so, a booted foot kicked the door wide open to admit two uniformed black policemen and a white man in civilian clothes. The uniformed men stood blocking the door, while the other man made hastily for the window and stood in front of it.

"Are you Philemon Dlamini?" he asked. When Philemon nodded, the white man continued. "I am Sergeant Erasmus, Security Police. I have an order here, signed by the Minister of Justice, authorizing your detention for an indefinite period. Get your clothes and come with me."

"What!" exclaimed Philemon. "I haven't done anything you can arrest me for. What are you talking about?"

"Don't be bloody stupid, kaffir," replied Erasmus. "Under the security laws I don't have to give you a reason. And I'm not arresting you; I'm detaining you. There's a big difference. Let me explain what it is. We don't take you to court and you don't see an attorney."

He walked over to the bed, hooked his foot under it and kicked it over. "Now hurry up and collect your rubbish before I break something."

Despondently Philemon walked to his bed, righted it and picked up his suitcase. "This is all the rubbish I've got."

"Don't be cheeky," said the white man, grabbing Philemon by the arm and trying to spin him around.

Philemon wrenched his arm free. "Take your hands off me," he shouted.

Faster than a breath could be drawn, the two black policemen grabbed Philemon's arms and held him securely, while the white man stepped back. Without taking his eyes off Philemon, Erasmus ordered the prisoner to be taken away.

Outside in the dark street, Philemon was ordered into the back of a white Ford Escort and found himself cramped between the two uniformed policemen, while the white man climbed behind the wheel in front. Philemon's knees almost touched the roof of the car and he clutched his belongings uncomfortably on his lap. They left the township silently, enveloped in dust thrown up by the car. Occasionally the driver glared at Philemon in the rear view mirror, but not a word was spoken until they arrived at a dark, two-storey building in the city.

As the car pulled into an enclosed courtyard, Philemon was ordered out and escorted into the brightly lit interior of the building. There was an ominous hush in the long corridor where he found himself. Even when a fourth policeman joined the escort party leading Philemon to an unknown destination, the only sound was of their marching feet. Suddenly Erasmus came to a stop and pressed a button on the wall. An inconspicuous door slid open to reveal an elevator into which his escorts shoved Philemon. He could sense that they were descending a few floors until they came to an abrupt stop with a bump. Once again he found himself moved along a corridor until they reached a cell marked C17. The Sergeant fiddled clumsily with a bunch of keys until he found the right one and opened the door. He stood aside and Philemon was unceremoniously pushed inside. Caught unawares, he stumbled forward and fell. As he struggled to his feet, he saw the Sergeant grab the suitcase and back out of the room saying, "Get up, kaffir. I didn't say you could sit down. You stand there and wait until I get back."

With that he slammed the door shut and locked it. Philemon was left on his own.

****

The events in the early hours of that morning had not gone unnoticed. Simon Gumede lived in the room next to Philemon in Kwa Mashu, and he was also awakened by the loud banging at four o' clock. Unlike Philemon, he hadn't experienced enough raids to take it calmly when he heard the police identify themselves. His instinct was to run, but knowing he wouldn't be able to get past them, he crept quietly to his door and listened. The walls in the hostel were very thin, so it was easy to hear what was being said next door. When he heard that these were Security Police, Simon's heart constricted with fear for his friend. He heard a man's voice tell Philemon that he was being detained without an attorney, and without going to court. Opening his door just a crack, he peeped through into the hallway and saw that it was empty. He knew that he needed to get help fast. Without making a sound he opened his door and just as he heard a loud crash from something falling over, he made a break and slipped out of his room. The noise from Philemon's room gave him cover to bolt outside the main door of the building unnoticed. He saw a white car parked in the street and crept cautiously away around the corner of the house, before sprinting to hide behind a shanty on the opposite side of the road. Here he watched to see what would happen, his heart thumping. It was only a few minutes later that his friend emerged with two policemen and a white man, and was pushed into the car. There was just enough light and time for Simon to note the number plate before the car drove off in a cloud of choking dust. He scratched the registration number into the sand. ND 114-6529.

Chapter 10

On that fateful night in November, Helen felt uneasy saying goodbye to Al. Going into Kwa Mashu was a journey into the unknown for any white South African and she felt apprehensive about his safety. She rang Mary to calm her nerves before going to visit her parents. They had become very close friends in their first year at university when they had been in the same residence. Mary was very extroverted and took pity on the shy Afrikaans girl in the room next door, renaming her H.A. Mary's warmth soon melted her new friend's reserve and H.A. experienced fun and adventure that she'd never been exposed to before. However, when they went on demonstration marches after student leaders had been detained under house arrest, or even worse, had been imprisoned for ninety days without trial, Mary had been calm and determined in her pursuit of justice. Helen had learned to be bold and ignore the plainclothes policemen as they tried to mingle in the crowd and take surreptitious photos.

She listened to Mary laugh now, advising her to avoid arguments with her father. "When you two are married and have the first kid, the old boy will accept everything. Just keep on smiling sweetly and carry on doing what you want to do. And don't worry about Al, he knows how to look after himself."

H.A. put her brooding thoughts aside and climbed into her old gray Volkswagen Beetle to visit her parents, determined to keep her temper in check and not be drawn into an argument about politics or Alan. That was the way that every topic of conversation went with her Father these days. She had a knot in her stomach as she parked her car and heard Wagter barking at her. As she opened the gate, he began jumping up to greet her, wagging his tail. She wished her father could be as welcoming as his dog, but he only knew how to be the watchdog and protector, not the playful hound, she thought to herself.

She found her mother in the kitchen and they embraced warmly, happy to see one another. Engela Du Toit inspected her daughter to see whether she was looking healthy. "You have black rings under your eyes Helena. Are you working too hard and not getting enough sleep?" she asked anxiously.

"Oh Mom, it's busy at the end of the school year, but it'll be over soon and then I'll have six weeks to sleep!" her daughter laughed. "How are you though? And where's Pa?"

"He's in the front room, my angel. He seems upset about something, I don't know what. He won't say. He's also been working too hard. Maybe he'll cheer up if you go and talk to him. You go and do that while I make some coffee for all of us."

Unsuspectingly, H.A. walked into the room where her father was sitting glumly in his chair, sucking his pipe and reading his paper. He didn't look up and she wondered whether he hadn't heard her, or whether he was simply being difficult. Trying to stick to her good intentions of making an effort, she came up behind his chair and playfully covered his eyes with her hands.

"Dammit, can't you see I'm reading!" he growled.

Taken aback, she dropped her hands. Still he didn't look at her, but continued reading his paper.

"Pa, it's me, Helena," she said.

Still he said nothing.

Hurt gave way to anger and her vow to keep her temper was forgotten. "What's got into you? It's not very pleasant coming to see you if you're going to behave like this," she remonstrated.

Captain Du Toit put down his paper, rose from his chair and turned to confront her. "Don't talk to me like that, do you hear? You have the cheek to talk about my behavior! I am disgusted with your's," he snapped.

"Mine?" she gasped. "Excuse me, but what have I done?"

"You are behaving like, like - like a cheap slut!" he said, going quite red in the face. "You said you were going to be living with Mary. Do you think I don't know who's really living in that apartment with you? And do you think I don't know all about him and his friends?"

"Pa," she gasped. "How dare you say that? This is the seventies, not the Dark Ages. Things have changed since you and Ma were young and there's nothing cheap in my behavior. It's your mind that sees it that way. Alan and I love each other and we're going to spend the rest of our lives together, and what happens between us is our business, not yours."

"Some things never change, Helena," he shouted angrily. "Common decency stays the same. It's not just that you're sleeping with this bastard, it's the sort of man that he is."

She frowned defensively as he continued.

"He's a communist and he mixes with blacks, and before long he's going to land himself in serious trouble."

"He is not a communist and who cares if he has black friends? So do I and do you know what, they...."

"And before long you'll also land yourself in serious trouble, along with him and his friends," he interrupted. " I'm telling you, Helena, then there'll be nothing I can do to help you, so you'd better listen to me. Forget this man. Leave him and come home now."

"You're mad," she gasped. "You're quite insane. I love Alan and I would never leave him. This is the man I'm going to marry next year. He's the finest man I've ever known," she said pointedly. "And one of the things I love about him most is that he cares about all people, not just white ones, or Afrikaans ones."

"Do you know where he is tonight?" he demanded suddenly.

She looked at him cautiously. "Working," she replied.

"Like hell he's working," he snorted. "The finest man you've ever known is in Kwa Mashu, looking for trouble. Yes he's working all right, with a communist who's inciting people to violence. We'll see how much he cares about all these people after this, if he's lucky enough to get out of there alive. I don't think they'll be too pleased to see his white face amongst them. They'll probably stab first and ask questions later."

"How do you know all this?" asked Helen coldly.

"Do you think I was born yesterday? We have our ways of finding out things that concern the security of the state and the people. That's why we're the Security Police."

"The only security you're concerned with is your own," she retorted. "Don't you think you're lacking in the common decency you talk of, invading people's privacy? It's despicable."

"Helena, sit down and listen to your father." He took her firmly by the arm and sat her down in a chair next to him. She sat stiffly clutching the arms of the chair as he seated himself and tapped his pipe in a large ashtray, before stuffing it with tobacco again and lighting up with a few long sucks. He cleared his throat as he searched for words.

"My angel, you've always been such a joy to your mother and me and it's because we love you that we're concerned about you. You're making a big mistake and we're very worried that you are ruining your life." He shifted in his seat and cleared his throat again. "There are many things that are hard to accept when you're young and you think you're in love. Believe it or not, I was young once too! But love is much more than desire. Desire doesn't last long. It takes your fancy for a while and then it burns itself out very quickly. Love is different. It lasts forever because it goes hand in hand with respect and caring." He sucked thoughtfully on his pipe. "Ask yourself now if you can really respect this man's values, Helena. For a start, he's not an Afrikaner so he doesn't share your background and all the values you've grown up with. And then, doesn't it make you worry that he's so friendly with blacks? Is there something wrong with him that he can't find white friends?"

Helen was sobbing, shaking her head in her hands. "I don't want to hear any more. Stop it. We always end up arguing and I really don't want to. Please can't we just talk about other things?"

"Agh, I'm sorry, my angel, but the truth is painful. It's hard to see because you find this man very attractive. I understand that. But you have to face up to the truth and deal with it," he said, patting her hand. "This is not the right man for you. If he cared for you, he wouldn't endanger you as he does. No, he wouldn't, he'd want to protect you. You're young and beautiful. You'll get over him and find somebody else who will look after you and be a good father to your children one day. Believe me. You'll be thankful when you look back. You've made some mistakes that I wish you hadn't made. But you know, it's never too late to mend your ways."

She cried into her hands, trying to control herself. After a while she looked up at him with tears streaming down her face. He ached seeing her unhappiness and tried to comfort her saying, "Here's a tissue, blow your nose and stop crying now. He's not worth your tears, my angel. One of the most difficult things in life is confronting your mistakes and fixing them. Some people never learn to do that because they're too proud - and that's a sin. You just be strong for me and everything is going to be alright."

Her voice was strained as she replied, "You just don't understand, Pa. It's you who needs to look at your mistakes. I'm not crying for him, Pa, I'm crying for you." She blew her nose and looked him straight in the eyes. "Let me say again, I love Alan, I intend to marry him with or without your permission. I would prefer to have your blessing, but if I don't have it, it won't stop me. I'm an adult, not a child - this is my decision and my life. "

His head jerked forward and he gaped with astonishment.

"The values that you speak of aren't mine," she continued. "You scorn anybody that doesn't think like you and I won't be like that. I can't understand how you can call yourself a Christian and still

73

believe that someone is worth less than you because they speak a different language, or their skin is a different color. I'm sorry, Pa, but I can't respect you until you learn to respect the rights of everybody in this country." Her voice choked as she sobbed, "You are ruining my life, and the lives of everyone in South Africa."

"How dare you speak to me like that!" he shouted. "How dare you! I brought you up teaching you to honor your mother and father. Everything you're doing now brings us dishonor. You're breaking the commandments, and living in sin."

"What about the commandment that says 'Love thy neighbor?' or 'Do unto others as you would them do unto you?' Do you think you do that?" she said archly. "You think I'm living in sin? Christ Almighty, you are steeped in sin and you can't even see it."

"And now you think you're so clever you can take the Lord's name in vain. Do you still believe in any of the commandments or do you make up your own? I am ashamed of you, Helena."

They stared angrily at one another. Each wanted to change the other's point of view, but neither was able to move an inch. Finally Captain Du Toit picked up his newspaper and returned to his chair. "Get out of here, do you hear me? Get out and don't come back into this house until you've mended your ways. You're no daughter of mine until you do."

She stood staring at him in disbelief. "You don't mean that Pa," she said, "you'll regret that you said that."

His enraged face contorted as he shouted, "GET OUT!"

It would be a long time before he would see her again. Helen ran into the kitchen and sobbed on her mother's shoulder, like a child. Neither woman said anything: the older because she didn't realize the gravity of the situation, and the younger because she did. She drove home through blinding tears to await Alan's return. "Oh God," she pleaded, "Please let him be safe. Please."

Two hours seemed like two years as she paced the room, listening to the clock ticking. She tried to call Mary but there was no reply. Several times she thought she heard Al coming up the stairs, then finally she heard the key in the door and ran to open it, almost singing with relief. As she hugged him, he fondled her hair saying, "It's good to be home, H.A. That's a disturbing place. Hell, you can't imagine that such poverty exists."

He told her about the meeting and his feelings in Kwa Mashu. She listened to the compassion in him and wished her father could have some of it. When he had finished describing his experience, she told him of the argument with her father, and found the support she needed after hours of torment.

"So they're tailing us. I might have guessed. That doesn't bother me too much because I haven't got anything to hide. In fact we could have some fun," he laughed. "You know my love, if your father has any guts, and if he's anything like his daughter he has got guts, he'll think about what you said to him. Let's hope he changes his views, or at least that he comes to respect yours." He kissed her again. "Thank you for loving me so much. I love you more than anything I've ever known."

He drew her closer and gazed into her eyes, as if seeing her for the first time. Her lips parted to speak, but before she could do so he covered her mouth with his own, and then her body with his as they sank onto the sofa. They found solace from the hell that each had experienced that night, and then a welcome oblivion.

Chapter 11

Al and Helen were sound asleep at six o'clock on the third of November 1973, when H.A. was awakened by an urgent knocking on the front door. She lay for a moment, hoping Al would get up first, but one look at him showed he hadn't stirred. Wrapping a robe around herself, she ran to the door and looked through the peephole before opening it, wondering who could be so insistent about waking them this early. She looked in surprise at the distraught young black man in front of her and asked cautiously, "What do you want?"

"Ma'm, I'm looking for Mr. Griffin. He knows me. My name is Simon. I must speak to him, please."

"Wait there, I'll call him," she said, noticing how the young man glanced nervously over his shoulder.

Al was already getting out of bed to see what was happening when she got to the bedroom. "What's going on?"

"Someone to see you. Simon. Says you know him."

"Simon? Who the hell is he?" he muttered, annoyed at being awoken. Striding to the front door he pulled it open and then his face softened at the sight of the distraught young man. He recognized him from the Kwa Mashu Committee the previous night. Putting his hand

76

out to Simon, he invited him inside and asked what was troubling him.

"It's Philemon, Mr. Griffin. Early this morning, before the sun was up, some policemen came to our hostel and I saw them take him away."

"What!" exclaimed Al. He looked at Helen and rubbed the stubble on his chin. "I can't believe they would do this. Simon, come in and tell me all you know."

Simon looked relieved to be safely inside and stopped looking so anxiously over his shoulder. He seemed very close to tears though, so Al settled him at the kitchen table with tea and some toast and jam, which he ate ravenously. At first they all felt awkward, sitting around the same table eating breakfast, but as Al began to question Simon, their thoughts concentrated on Philemon's plight and their own unusual circumstances became unimportant.

"Simon," Al said, "I want you to tell me everything you saw and heard. Take your time, but don't leave anything out because it might be vital. Did you hear what they've charged him with?"

"I heard one of the policeman say that they didn't have to give reasons. It was the white man who said that. I think he also said that Philemon wasn't going to court."

Slowly Simon recounted the terrible happenings of the morning, right from the first loud banging. As he finished his story, he thrust his hand into his shirt pocket and drew out a scrap of paper. "That's the number of the white car. I copied it from where I wrote it in the sand as soon as I could."

"You've done well Simon. It's very good that you've given us all this information, and it's good that you came straight to me. We need to track down that car registration, but I think there'll be no surprises. He's been taken away by the Security Police, without a doubt. The bastards." With that Al sprang into action. "Let me get hold of the Legal Group right away. We've got to find where they've taken him for starters."

While Alan was on the telephone, Simon continued eating his breakfast. He was hungry and weary, and his head throbbed with anxiety. "Philemon is a good man," he said to himself, "I don't understand why anyone would do this to him. He's done nothing wrong. Why do they want to lock him up?"

He hadn't realized that he'd been speaking to an audience until he heard Helen say softly, "I don't know, Simon, I don't understand it any more than you do. I don't know what to say."

He looked away from her with embarrassment, unused to being addressed by a white woman. He said clumsily, "Thank you for the food, Ma'm. I must go now. Please thank Mr. Griffin for me. This is my address if he needs to speak to me again." He wrote the information down and then thanked her again, before heading out the door with his thoughts still racing.

He rushed to get back to Kwa Mashu and tell the other committee members what had happened since last night, but his thoughts kept returning to his encounter with Sipu and Joe. He thought of them saying that Philemon was a toothless dog, and it angered him. "If he has no bite, then why would the police put him in prison? He hasn't done anything wrong, so the reason they've taken him away must be because they are afraid of him. Philemon is right, I know he is," he kept saying to himself. "We won't achieve anything with violence. Sipu and Joe say that we have nothing to lose, but that's not true. We'll lose our lives. Mr. Griffin will find Philemon and protect him. I trust him, and most of all I trust Philemon." He walked with greater assurance as he re-affirmed his belief in his mentor. "If those guys try to talk badly about him again, I'll tell them I don't believe them and they must leave me alone. I don't want to think about their ideas any more, but I really felt like killing those policemen this morning. Maybe if I'd had a gun I would even have done so!" He was startled by this realization and quickly dismissed the troubling thought. "I must get to Reverend Mkize."

Chapter 12

At first Philemon stared with blazing eyes at the slammed door, focusing on the four-inch square observation hatch positioned at eye-level. Then he took a deep breath and turned to look at his surroundings, which were grim and bleak. He was in a small concrete room with no windows or furniture. In a far corner lay a single khaki blanket, and above him was a sturdy, timber beam running across the width of the cell, a few inches below the concrete ceiling. Next to it was an unshaded light bulb that caused a sinister shadow to fall across the room.

With a single stride Philemon sprang at the door and beat it with his huge fists. His pounding echoed back at him, but otherwise there was no reaction from anywhere. His hands stretched out and began to feel the surface of the door, which was smooth and flush with the wall. The observation hatch too, was flush with the door, offering no possibility of a handhold. He turned and sat dejectedly on the blanket. His frustration and helplessness filled him like a raging flood. He had no outlet other than to ineffectually pound his fist on the floor and stamp his foot. He remained isolated interminably and began to panic that he'd been forgotten. Nobody who cared even knew he was here. His mouth was dry and his head ached. Eventually he dozed in and out of fretful dreams, which were easier than the nightmare of being awake.

Some hours later he was awakened by the metallic jarring of a key turning in the lock. The door swung open to reveal a white man in khaki prison warder's uniform, swinging a pair of handcuffs and laughing humorlessly. He was a large man, about the same height as Philemon, but covered with more excess flesh than muscle. His stomach strained against his belt and hung over the top of it. His fair hair was shaven short to the scalp, and his bloated, florid face rested fluidly above a series of chins.

"I'm Warder Van Zyl and I'll be in charge of you until you're released - if you're released," he said gruffly as he entered the room. "You're going to see the Captain now and you're going to show him respect. I'm going to put these handcuffs on you." He held them up in front of Philemon's face and rattled them. Two other white warders entered the cell and stood firmly behind Van Zyl, who addressed Philemon again. "Are you going to put them on quietly, or are we going to beat you up first?"

Philemon slowly got to his feet and stood next to the Warder with his arms outstretched, saying nothing except with his eyes. The handcuffs were swiftly snapped into place and he was pushed into the corridor. Van Zyl poked him roughly in the chest, "Listen, you black bastard, follow me and don't give any trouble. You might be big, but the three of us will knock the shit out of you so fast you won't know which end is up."

The four figures marched briskly along the corridor and into the waiting elevator. As the doors closed behind them, Van Zyl pushed the middle button. It surprised Philemon to see only three buttons, as he had the impression that previously they'd descended further. He dismissed the thought as the door opened again at the ground floor. The courtyard outside was visible and as he was marched further down the corridor, he could hear and see traffic through the barred windows. It calmed him momentarily to see some semblance of normality and the outside world. It seemed so close he could almost touch it.

They stopped outside a closed door on which Warder Van Zyl rapped sharply. A loud voice bellowed "Enter," and Philemon found himself face to face with the Captain, who was seated at his desk.

"Bantu prisoner, Philemon Dlamini, sir, handcuffed and ready for questioning," intoned Warder Van Zyl.

The Captain stood up and moved around his desk slowly, sizing up the prisoner and staring piercingly into his eyes. "I am Captain Du Toit. You already know your Warder, and this is Sergeant Erasmus who is standing behind you. Now you are going to answer a few questions for us."

"I won't answer anything without my attorney present," answered Philemon.

Van Zyl, who was standing next to the prisoner, punched him in the stomach. Philemon didn't flinch but turned slowly to face the man who was smiling broadly at him. With the speed of a striking mamba, the black man swung his manacled hands up and locked them at the back of the Warder's neck. Swiftly the two armed guards raised their rifles and jammed them painfully into Philemon's ribs. The prisoner gave one last squeeze with his hands, causing the steel handcuffs to bite into the Warder's purpling throat, and then he let go. Van Zyl fell to the floor, gasping air into his lungs and rubbing his bruised neck.

Neither the Captain nor the Sergeant tried to help the stricken Warder, but simply watched like spectators at a sporting match. Captain Du Toit turned to Philemon with a raised eyebrow, and said, "That was a stupid thing to do. This man is going to be in control of your life for quite a long time, Philemon. You're at his mercy, you know." He returned to the seat at his desk, and the Sergeant sat down too. Van Zyl struggled to his feet and glared venomously at the black man, with the two guards now stationed next to him.

The Captain began to speak. "You can't see your attorney, boy. You're being detained under the Terrorism Act and you're not entitled to one. As I said before, you are here to answer some questions and the sooner you do so, the sooner we can let you go. It doesn't matter to us; we've got all the time in the world. If you're stubborn, Warder Van Zyl will tie you up and then ask you some questions, but believe me, we will have answers from you. And by the way," he said, reaching for his pipe, "your friend, Alan Griffin, is a good friend of mine too. In fact, he's going to marry my daughter. Small world isn't it! He's been very helpful. Very helpful." He inhaled on his pipe and sat back in his chair, placing his feet on the desk.

Philemon was shocked to hear this, but he tried not to show any reaction.

"I think you will realize," continued the Captain, "that there's very little I don't know about you. I have details of all the meetings of your committee since you formed it, and all your resolutions. You got the bus boycott going some years ago, didn't you? This Reverend Mkize must get a bit annoying when he disagrees with you so much. He's much more moderate than you, isn't he?" A veteran interrogator, the Captain paused to let the impact of his inside information unnerve Philemon.

"If you know so much about me and my committee, why do you need to ask me questions?" scoffed Philemon.

"You're very clever aren't you! You're right, I know the answers already, so what I want from you is a confession. Let's get right to the point."

"Confession? What do you want me to say? Forgive me, Captain, for I have sinned. I'm not a Catholic, I confess my sins privately to God."

"Oh, this boy is very clever, isn't he! But did you hear that, he's just admitted that he has something to confess. I'm afraid nothing is private for you now, Philemon. If you take a crap, I'm going to know about it. So let's hear what you have to confess."

"My conscience is clear, I have nothing to confess."

Captain Du Toit tapped his pipe in an ashtray. "Philemon, can you stand pain? Not just the pain of falling, or being hit in a fight; but real pain, slowly and systematically applied by a professional? I wonder."

Sergeant Erasmus stood up, put his hands in his pockets and approached Philemon. "I've been talking to your committee member, Simon Gumede, and he tells me that you've been trying to incite him and other Committee members to break the law. You've been trying to cause a confrontation with the police." He kept out of Philemon's arm range, but stepped a bit closer to him. "Why don't you avoid a lot of unnecessary pain and trouble for yourself, and confess that you're an agitator and a communist?"

The Captain added, "Please don't think that we enjoy causing you pain. But we have to protect this country from violence and anarchy. That's what we're here to do."

"I've never tried to incite anyone to break the law. Never. I've always been against confrontation and I'm not a communist. I swear to you, I'm not." He felt dejected and confused, and desperately wanted time to sort out his thoughts. He looked at the Captain and said, "You obviously know a lot about me and I can see there's no use trying to hide anything from you, but I would first like to think what I'm going to say."

"As I said before Philemon, we have all the time in the world. You appear to be more co-operative now, so I'll give you half an hour to think about your confession. It'd better be good, otherwise you're not going to like the consequences." He nodded to Van Zyl, who promptly ordered Philemon and the guards to follow him.

They marched down the corridor into the elevator, where the door shut with a clang. Philemon stared at the control panel as the Warder appeared to press on the metal below the last button. They started to descend and the Warder moved his hand away quickly. "What are you staring at, Kaffir?" he snarled at Philemon. Philemon looked away and said nothing.

"You're learning to keep your cheeky mouth shut. Good." He rubbed his neck and glared at Philemon, adding, "I hope you don't confess just yet. I want to enjoy watching you suffer."

As the door of his cell closed behind him, Philemon collapsed onto the blanket. He took a deep breath and tried to clear his brain. "It's a terrible thing to be betrayed by friends," he thought. "I would never have believed Alan Griffin would be a traitor. It doesn't make sense though. He is doing so much for my people, why would he do this to me? Unless the Security Police are paying his costs and it's all just a big front. That's it! That must be it. They pay him, he puts up a front to help us, and then he infiltrates the people he's supposed to be helping."

There was still a nagging doubt though. "Why go to all that trouble with him, when they obviously have a plant on the Committee already? They must be paying Simon too. Suddenly he's got three jobs, not two!" He sat up with a start. "No. It's not Simon. He's only been on the committee a couple of months, but they spoke of knowing everything since it started. They lied about Simon. They're trying to confuse me and make me lose faith. If they lied about Simon, I'm sure they lied about Alan. They're not telling me who the informer is; they're trying to throw me off the scent. Alan doesn't know me very well anyway. He knows as much about me as all the people at that meeting last night. My God, was it only last night?" His thoughts were beginning to make sense to him at last. "They have an informer on the committee, or even someone in the next room at Mama Gloria's, pretending to be a beer drinker, listening all the while near the door. Maybe even Mama Gloria! But it's not Alan or Simon giving them information. It's someone else."

Philemon waited with nerves on edge for his captors to fetch him again. The minutes turned to hours, and he was given nothing to eat or drink, nor any toilet facilities. He began to feel light-headed from hunger, his mouth was parched, and he needed to relieve himself. Nobody came.

Suddenly the light in his cell went out and he was thrown into total darkness. He was stunned by the impenetrable blackness and silence. He stood up slowly, so as not to lose his bearings, and with his eyes fixed on where he knew the door to be, made his way across the concrete floor. When he collided with a hard surface, he moved his flat palms across it until he could feel the smooth texture of the door next to the roughness of the wall. Keeping his hands pressed against this link with outside, he slowly lowered himself to the floor, where he thought he could feel a slight draft. He lay down with the side of his face on the floor and discovered a small thread of light, just visible. This brought a surge of relief and he lay in that position for a while until the discomfort from his bladder became unbearable. Desperately, he brought his knees up underneath him and knelt so that his eyes never moved from the tiny fragment of light. In this prayer-like attitude, he said out loud, "I am the way, and the truth, and the light," and then slowly he began to recite the twenty-third Psalm to himself, saying repeatedly, "Yea though I walk through the Valley of Death, I shall fear no evil."

He began feeling desperate to urinate, and no matter how he lay or sat, he was unable to relieve the pressure in his bladder. He considered relieving himself in a corner, but feared the smell would become disgusting before long, and he had a sense that his captors were trying to force him to lose his dignity in this way. "I won't let them win," he thought defiantly, "but I must get my blanket and stay warm."

He moved his head around until he was able to ascertain where the corner of the room was, and then on his hands and knees he crawled backwards, with his eyes still fixed on the light. As he moved backwards, the light became fainter until it disappeared completely. Panic-stricken, he threw himself forward on his stomach and even though pain shot through him as he hit the ground, he could see the light again. "I must stop being so stupid," he chided himself. "The light isn't going away, it's just me moving away from it. Now get the bloody blanket quickly and get back to the door. That light's still going to be there." He continued crawling backwards, keeping his eyes fixed on the place where he had last seen the light. He reached the corner where his hands groped until they felt the warmth of the blanket. He grasped it tightly, threw it over his shoulder and methodically made his way back to the light, which reappeared, as he knew it would.

As the panic receded and he relaxed, he became aware of his bladder once more. "Look at the light," he told himself, "think about something else. Don't think about peeing."

His mind drifted to his family, and he tried to picture his wife, Frieda, as she stirred porridge for their breakfast in her big, three-legged pot, with the chickens scratching in the dirt around her. He could almost smell the wood smoke as he imagined her stirring a glowing log with her foot, sending sparks flying as the log moved deeper into the fire. He could picture Nkosinati sitting cross-legged and waiting patiently for his meal. He remembered how his little boy loved to sing and it brought tears to his eyes. He longed to be there, watching the sugar cane blowing like long, rolling waves around their huts, and feeling the red earth beneath his bare feet. He felt a little comfort, knowing that the Committee would try to help Frieda with money until he was free again.

"Dear God, let that be soon," he prayed.

He wondered whether he would lose his job at Frazer's. Tears rolled down his cheeks as he lay motionless, trying to ignore the ache in his abdomen. The tears were for his family and the uncertainty of their future. Finally, he slept fitfully, awakened many times by the pain. He forced himself to remain still every time he awoke, and look for the thread of light. It was always reassuringly there.

All of a sudden he was awakened by the brightness of the overhead light coming on in his room. Startled, he jumped to his feet and rubbed his eyes. As he stood, the pain in his bladder hit him like a blow and he writhed in agony, sinking to the ground again. He heard the door opening and the voice of Warder Van Zyl saying, "Come on Kaffir, it's party time. We've got some nice treats in store for you. On your feet, let's go." As he raised himself, Philemon felt wetness on the front of his pants. He stood up to his full height and glanced down at the wet patch. "It's only a few drops," he thought. "I'm sure I can hold out."

Van Zyl had also noticed. "Well, well. Look what an effect we had on him," he laughed to the guards. "He got such a fright he pissed his pants. If you thought that was scary Kaffir, just wait!" He marched into the cell with the armed guards, and ordered Philemon to put his hands out for handcuffs. Once they were snapped in place, he led the march back into the elevator, chuckling to himself. Again

Philemon had the sensation of ascending further than the panel indicated, but he didn't have time to think about it before they arrived back in the Captain's office.

"Good morning Philemon," Captain Du Toit said, "I hope you had a good night's sleep and feel refreshed. You're ready to prepare and sign your confession, I trust?"

"Before I can do anything, I need to go to the toilet," he responded.

"Van Zyl, this should have been done beforehand. Escort the prisoner to the toilet," the Captain ordered angrily.

The relief of emptying his bladder and bowels was enormous and he felt quite weak at the end of it. He wryly thought of asking Van Zyl to wipe his backside for him, as the Warder wouldn't remove the handcuffs. He washed his hands as best he could and drank thirstily, splashing water around his face and neck as he did so. He was about to leave but quickly turned to drink again. Like a camel, he tried to store water, until he cursed inwardly, realizing that what went in would have to come out rather than being stored. Finally, feeling a bit refreshed but still very hungry, he was marched back to face the Captain.

"The Sergeant isn't here yet, but I think we can start without him," Captain Du Toit said crisply. "What have you decided to tell us? Please sit down."

Cautiously Philemon sat down. He didn't trust the apparent politeness, and suspected the Captain's demeanor could change as swiftly as a stalking lion could spring.

"What I told you before, I haven't broken any laws, I am not a communist, and I don't believe in violent confrontation. I'm trying to help my people who have very hard lives. That's all I can say. You have no evidence against me."

The Captain sniffed loudly and then reached for his pipe and matches. The door opened and Sergeant Erasmus slipped quietly into the room. Captain Du Toit carefully and deliberately lit his pipe and watched the smoke coil up to the ceiling. There it hung like the silence. Eventually he said, "Sergeant, Philemon has decided that he has nothing to confess." He turned his steely gaze back to the prisoner and said, "What makes you think we have no evidence against you?"

"If you had any, you would charge me. Instead you've locked me up, you won't let me see my attorney, and you want to force something out of me. That's what the Terrorism Act is for, isn't it?" replied Philemon.

"Believe me, we will force something out of you." The Captain replaced his pipe in the ashtray and exhaled deeply, blowing smoke into Philemon's face. He walked unhurriedly around his desk and turned to the Warder saying, "Tie him to the chair."

Philemon knew it was useless to resist, so he sat docilely while Van Zyl slipped a rope around his arms and pulled a tight knot. The rope was then wound around him and the chair like a cocoon, and pulled tight again until it cut painfully into him. After this, his legs were strapped to the chair and lashed securely. The Captain examined the trussed victim before returning to his seat, where he fixed his eyes on the prisoner. "Van Zyl, no mess in my office. If it's going to get messy, take him to the interrogation room. Erasmus, you ask the questions."

The Sergeant had not moved since entering the office, but now he walked over to the desk and sat on it, beckoning one of the Warders to come closer as he did so. "Now, Mr. Dlamini, tell me how many times you've been out of the country?" he asked in a mild tone.

"I refuse to answer any questions without my attorney present," replied Philemon, looking straight ahead.

Erasmus clicked his tongue disapprovingly. "You know that's not going to happen. I'm trying to help you because if you don't answer my questions truthfully and completely, Warder Van Zyl is going to hurt you. Let me ask you again, where were you trained? Was it Moscow or Beijing?"

Philemon continued to gaze at a point on the Captain's pocket and remained silent. Behind him, the Warder took a rifle from one of the guards.

"Philemon," continued the Sergeant, "if you don't co-operate, you're going to get hurt. Now, where do your instructions come from, Moscow or Beijing?"

"I've told you. I talk to God and my conscience. That's where my instructions come from." He kept his eyes fixed on the same spot.

Suddenly pain exploded in his back as the Warder rammed the rifle butt into Philemon's kidneys, shouting, "Answer, kaffir, or there's plenty more where that came from."

Philemon looked into the expressionless eyes of the Captain and then lowered his gaze, bracing himself for the next blow. This time it landed on the back of his neck, throwing his head forward. Lights flashed in front of his eyes and he felt bile rising in his throat. He struggled to control himself in front of that indifferent stare, but anger rose up in him and he spat venomously at the Captain's face. He watched with pleasure as spittle dripped from the bridge of Du Toit's nose, and disgust blazed in the interrogator's previously blank stare. His pleasure was short-lived as blows rained down on him from all sides. His chair toppled over as the Warder and two guards continued pounding him, even though he had lost consciousness when his head struck the floor.

The mist around him was impenetrable as he struggled back to consciousness. Nausea broke over him in waves and he retched dryly. He could feel hard, cold concrete beneath him and when his vision finally cleared, he could see that he was back in his cell. Cautiously he tried to push himself into a sitting position but his arms were unsteady and he slipped, falling into a sticky pool of blood. He lay gasping for breath with the metal handcuffs still biting into his wrists. The shock of the slight fall made him sob with frustration and he felt his stomach heave involuntarily.

Suddenly he heard the loud grating of the steel door being unlocked and looked up to see the gloating face of his warder. "Not feeling so good today, Kaffir? Well I've brought a doctor to have a look at you."

The Warder moved aside to reveal a nervous, gray-haired man in a white coat, who quickly knelt beside Philemon and unbuttoned his patient's shirt. He requested the handcuffs to be removed so that he could carry out a swift examination with his stethoscope, and then gently prod the prisoner's battered body and head, noting the injuries and wounds. "This man has obviously been the victim of an assault," he said, closing his medical bag and dusting his knees as he stood up.

"Doctor, don't worry about what caused his problem. Just fix him up and don't ask questions."

The medic looked distastefully at the Warder and continued, "The patient has two broken ribs on his right side; he has suffered a heavy blow to the back of his head that needs to be x-rayed; his body is badly bruised and cut, and he's concussed. He needs to be hospitalized."

The Warder snorted derisively. "He's got more chance of getting pregnant! He's staying right where he is until he signs a piece of paper for us."

The doctor knelt once more and cleaned Philemon's wounds gently. When he was finished, he poured some water into a paper cup and gave it to his patient to drink. Then he produced a banana from his bag and said, "Eat this."

Van Zyl made an effort to snatch it away shouting, "What the hell! You're not here to feed the prisoner. What do you think you're doing?"

He was prevented by the doctor, who calmly held up his hand. "This is my patient and he needs to eat this immediately so that he can take some medicine, which should never be taken on an empty stomach. He's obviously not eaten for a considerable time. When he's had this medicine, I suggest you feed him properly, otherwise he'll become very ill and dehydrated." He proceeded to give Philemon some aspirin and a shot of morphine, before patting the prisoner sympathetically on the shoulder. "I'll check on you again," he said as he got up to leave.

"I don't think so," said Van Zyl, locking the door after him as they left, "you'll be called if you're needed. He's your patient when we ask you to look at him, but otherwise he's just a bloody prisoner! "

The Warder ordered one of the guards to bring some food, which was placed on the floor a few feet from Philemon. After dragging himself over to it, he discovered that it was a mug of water and a thick slice of stale brown bread. He cursed, but knew that he was going to need all his strength in the days ahead and so he forced himself to eat. He took small bites and chewed them well with a bit of water to soften the mouthful and wash it down. At first his stomach heaved, but it slowly began to settle with the bland food and he concentrated on keeping the bread down.

"I must stay strong," he told himself.

Chapter 13

John Msomi sat hunched over his can of beer in Mama Gloria's
eating-house. All too often he found solace in Mama's brew, and for
a few hours he forgot the pain he otherwise felt in his body and in his
heart. He welcomed the decline into stupor although he often grew
mournful along the way. There was always someone to talk to at
Mama Gloria's, and Toughy Khumalo often bought him beers to
make him feel better.

"You are too kind to me," he said, as Toughy put yet another drink
in front of him. He lifted the tin to his lips and drank deeply, spilling
and dribbling beer down his chin and onto his shirt. "Thank you, my
friend."

"I do it to make you happy, John. Tonight you seem very sad,
man. Tell me what's troubling you." The other man pulled up a
wooden box and sat down. "Have some more beer and tell me what's
wrong."

"I am very sad tonight, very sad. My friend has been taken away
by the police and I can't help him." He sniffed loudly and drank some
more beer. "He has always helped me, and now when he needs help,
I can do nothing. I'm no good to anyone."

"Don't be so hard on yourself, John. Tell me which friend this is who's in trouble."

"My friend Philemon."

"Oh, Philemon Dlamini?"

"Yes, my friend Philemon," moaned John Msomi. "The police have taken him away and nobody knows where he is."

"I can help you with that. Come, my friend, cheer up. I know people who can find out for us."

John Msomi was so excited that his hand started to shake. "You can find out where he is?" he asked, amazed.

"I think so. But you must help me a bit."

"Anything you want. I can get the Committee to help too."

"No!" snapped Toughy. "No, you mustn't do that." Seeing the startled look on John Msomi's face, he added reassuringly, "The fewer people trying to help, the less likely things will get messed up. Just the two of us will do this, and then we can tell the committee when we've found him. Okay?"

"Okay, I suppose so," agreed John.

"Do you remember where Philemon went last year when he went away? I remember you told me that he went on a trip."

"I don't remember where he went, somewhere far away. But I know it was the first of June, because it was my wife's birthday." He laughed to himself and had another sip of beer. "My wife is a beautiful woman, you know."

"I know she is, you're a lucky man. Philemon's lucky too, that he's got you for a friend. How long was he away?"

"A long time, too long. I remember he told us he would have to miss committee meetings for two months because he had some business to see to."

"That's a long time, you must have missed him, John. Want another beer?"

"You are very kind to me. When a man is worried, it's good to have a beer, but it's better when he has a good friend to buy it for him," he chuckled.

Toughy brought another drink and said to John, "Who's that man

93

that Philemon has made friends with? Not the attorney, the other man that he meets?"

"Oh, you mean Michael?"

"Yes, Michael. Why does Philemon meet him?"

"I don't know. He doesn't tell me everything." He gulped down some beer. "My wife makes good beer too. Better than this. I need to go back to my wife before she finds another man," he cried.

"John, don't be so tough on yourself. Your wife will wait for you, but you can't go back to her until you've helped Philemon. Remember?"

John nodded. "That's right, first I must do that."

"Maybe this friend Michael can help. Do you know his address so that I can contact him?" asked Toughy.

"No, I don't know. He lives in Johannesburg, you see. One day we were driving in the taxi together and we fetched him from the station to take him to our meeting."

"What did you talk about?"

"We talked about passbooks and stuff like that," he mumbled, smacking his lips after another big gulp. "I think they want to plan a big action to stop us carrying passbooks. You know like we did here. They want to do that everywhere. In Johannesburg, Pretoria, everywhere." He laughed happily. "That Philemon, he is very clever."

"He's a very clever man, John. I wonder where he and Michael get money from to do these things? It must cost a lot."

John Msomi sat staring into his beer thoughtfully. "I think Michael got some money somewhere. I remember he told us that the people overseas wanted to help us."

"What people overseas?"

"I don't know who they are, but Michael said money wasn't a problem."

"What else happened at that meeting?"

"I can ask Father Mkize, he'll remember. And he's got the minutes."

"No," said Toughy sternly, "remember, this is just you and me."

"But Father Mkize is good. He won't mess up," protested John.

"No. If you want me to help, then listen to me. Nobody else, do you understand? If the police discover we're trying to find Philemon, they'll move him. Then we'll be in big trouble too."

"How does it help Philemon if I find this out for you?" Msomi asked, suddenly suspicious.

"John Msomi! Can't you see that my friends need this information so that they can prove Philemon's innocence? Then they can persuade the police to release him. We know that Philemon is a good man, but we have to prove it to the police."

"Okay, okay. I'll look at those minutes if you want me to."

"That's good, John. You're a good friend. But remember, don't let anybody else know what we're doing yet." He patted him reassuringly, and said, "Maybe you should go to bed now. I'll walk with you. How quickly do you think you can take a look at those minutes?"

"Tomorrow maybe, if my head will wake up," he laughed.

"That's good. I'll buy you some more beer here tomorrow night and we can talk some more. Philemon will have a lot to thank you for," Toughy said, nodding his head.

Chapter 14

Philemon was awakened by the customary clang of the bolt being drawn and the door grating open. Warder Van Zyl strode into the cell, accompanied by two armed guards, and looked at Philemon's plate of unfinished food. "We must be over-feeding you, Kaffir," he exclaimed. Turning to a guard he shouted, "Halve his rations." He hunched his shoulders menacingly and glared at Philemon.

"Today you are going to make a full, signed confession, do you hear? There are two ways of doing it. Voluntarily, here in your cell, or with some help in the interrogation room. You choose!"

Philemon said nothing, but stared coldly at Van Zyl. The Warder glanced nervously at the guards behind him, then thrust his fist under the prisoner's chin, saying, "Make up your mind Kaffir. This is your last chance."

Philemon's gaze never faltered as he said, "Move your hand before I break your arm."

Van Zyl snapped his arm back and the guards stepped forward protectively. "For the last time, are you going to sign, or do we use force?"

Philemon slowly stood up and stretched to his full height,

thrusting his shoulders back and his chest out. Pain stabbed him from his cracked ribs, but he tried not to show it. "You'll have to use force. Which of you is the bravest? Your two guards look small and you look fat," he sneered.

"Do you want us to shoot you?"

"Your Captain won't like it if I'm dead. He needs me alive because he thinks I can tell him something."

Van Zyl's response was quick and vicious. "We won't shoot to kill, Kaffir, we'll shoot you in the knee. Very painful, but you'll be alive and ready to talk."

"You fat bastard, if you try to shoot me, you'd better shoot to kill, because I'll rip your throat out before your friends can even move a finger to help you." Philemon looked from one guard to the other, and then glared at the Warder.

The Warder stepped back in fright as the two guards directed their rifles at Philemon's knees. Van Zyl pulled a pistol from his pocket and in a flash fired a shot. The bullet whistled past the prisoner's head and gouged into the thick concrete wall next to him in a shower of cement shrapnel. Philemon's heart was racing.

"In future these stay on you," shouted Van Zyl, replacing the pistol and holding up handcuffs. "Much less trouble for us. Put your hands out Kaffir and keep your mouth shut. You've just made life very difficult for yourself. I really don't know why you always want to argue with me – you know you can't win."

Restrained in the handcuffs, Philemon was ordered down the corridor again, but instead of getting into the elevator, they entered an open door on the same floor. Once they were all inside, Van Zyl locked the door behind him. Sergeant Erasmus and two other white men were already in the room, waiting.

Philemon felt a cold shudder as he looked around the sinister dungeon. In the center of the room was a large, solid wooden table with leather straps lying across it. On one side of the table was a large concrete bath, and on the other were numerous chains with loops and straps hanging down at various heights from the ceiling. Further back in the room were a variety of steel instruments neatly arranged on shelves, alongside three machines with dials, wires and clamps resting on them. The room itself, like Philemon's cell, had no window, and was lit by a bare light bulb in the ceiling.

The faces of all the white men were completely expressionless, except for Van Zyl's. He looked eager and alert, excited by the events about to take place. Smiling maliciously he said, "Now you cheeky kaffir, we'll see if you're still so full of shit. Lie down," he ordered, pointing to the table.

Philemon took a step back towards the locked door and dropped to a crouched position, ready to spring. The six white men spread out in a semi-circle and silently began to move in on him. Philemon's heart was pounding in his ears as he helplessly watched the approaching onslaught. "Dear God," he prayed silently and fervently, "please help me."

The first blow was a kick in the side from one of the guards. "Get up on the table now," screamed Van Zyl, giving Philemon another kick, this time in the groin as he straightened up. This knocked the prisoner to the floor again, doubled up in pain. He looked up to see the Warder's bloated belly bouncing as he laughed obscenely. With pent up rage Philemon sprang, driving his huge, handcuffed fists full-force into the Warder's stomach. Air gushed out of the man's mouth like a suddenly deflated balloon, and he was thrown back against the table by the force of the blow.

In an instant Philemon was set upon by the other men, who pounded and kicked him mercilessly. He fought back like a wounded bull elephant, feeling his fists connecting with flesh many times, and his knees and feet striking hard against teeth and bones. He felt no pain as he lashed out in a desperate effort for survival, but the odds against him were too great and before long he found himself helplessly restrained.

As the other men climbed to their feet, rubbing various parts of their bodies and cursing, Van Zyl hooked one of the chains from the ceiling onto the handcuffs that bound Philemon. "Cheeky, fucking kaffir," muttered the Warder, slowly rubbing his neck and back. A trickle of blood ran down his cheek and his right eye looked swollen and discolored. He wiped the blood with the back of his hand and looked at it in disgust. "Right, that's it! You've just written your own sentence, you bastard." He stormed over to the machines and began viciously twisting dials and punching knobs.

The room was filled with the growl of a motor and suddenly the chain that was hooked to the handcuffs, began to grind upwards. Philemon was yanked to his feet and in slow motion his arms pulled up above him, followed by his body, until his fingers were almost touching the ceiling. He tried to grab the chain to take the weight off his wrists, but he felt his legs being held. Looking down he saw two guards holding him while another man removed his pants, before tying his feet together. Only when he was naked and bound, was he lowered to the floor and ordered to hop across to the table. As he looked at the cold surface, he was paralyzed with dread and despair, bemoaning the God who had forsaken him.

He was pushed forcibly onto the table where straps were quickly thrown across his body and tightened. The guards were swift and experienced, pinning him down as if he were a creature in a laboratory, ready for dissection, unable to move any part of his body. Terror washed in icy waves over his spine and forehead.

Two guards each took up a leather tjambok from the shelf and silently positioned themselves at the foot of the table. In unison, they began to strike the bottoms of his feet, slowly and systematically. At first it merely felt uncomfortable, but as time went on, the tenderness turned to pain. Another two men moved into position at his knees, and with the same slow, methodical rhythm, proceeded to strike his kneecaps. From time to time, the guards changed whips from one hand to the other, without missing a beat. Meanwhile the Warder wheeled a machine with electrical wires and clamps to the side of the table. Reaching down between the prisoner's legs he brutally clamped his victim's testicles, laughing as he did so.

"Now kaffir, this is the best part, hey. We'll try it here first, and then maybe we can give it a go on your dick. That'll stop your comings and goings, hey! How does that grab you?" He looked around at his colleagues and sniggered.

Sweat was bubbling up all over Philemon. The pain in his groin was intense, and his feet and knees felt on fire. He heard the Warder laughing coarsely and opened his eyes to see that bloated face positioned over his own, staring cruelly into his eyes like a monster from an old legend. "The Sergeant is going to ask you some questions now and you are going to give him satisfactory answers. Do you hear me? If you don't, your balls are going to fry."

The Sergeant glared at the Warder and then approached Philemon's head, standing just in the bound man's line of sight. "Answer my questions and you won't get hurt; we'll take all this off you. If you don't, well, you can see what's going to happen. The choice is up to you." He stared coldly. "Now tell me, who is your friend from Johannesburg?"

"I have lots of friends from Johannesburg," answered the prisoner.

A searing pain shot from his testicles, up through his stomach and forced a scream from his lips. His back arched from the shock, but just as suddenly the electricity was turned off and he lay groaning, whilst the hammering on his feet and knees continued relentlessly.

"Mind your manners, kaffir," shouted the Warder. "When you speak to this man you must call him Master."

"Philemon, you collected the man from the station and took him to Kwa Mashu by taxi. Who was he?" continued the interrogator.

"I don't know what you're talking about. I collect lots of people from the station in a taxi because I don't have a car," cried Philemon, quickly adding, "Master," as he saw a movement from the Warder.

"You are not co-operating Philemon. Do you want him to hurt you again?" asked Erasmus. "Let me refresh your memory for you. You picked this man up from the station and his first name was Michael. What was his last name?"

"I don't know, Master. I arranged the meeting with that man through the Kwa Mashu Committee. I can't remember now."

The Warder took another two wires and clipped them onto the black man's nipples, where they bit into the skin. As he did this, he said in a monotone, "Philemon, you're being very naughty. I'll have to jog your memory again." He flicked the switch and pain burst into the prisoner's body, forcing a strangled wail. He was left panting as the pain in his chest subsided.

"Did that get on your tits?" laughed the Warder.

Sergeant Erasmus snapped. "Shut up, Van Zyl, I don't want to hear any more of your bloody jokes. Just do your job. Work the machines when I indicate, otherwise shut up!" He turned his back on the Warder and concentrated his attention on the prisoner once more.

"This man Michael, I want to know his last name." A nod of the Sergeant's head produced another surge of pain through Philemon's body, burning his skin and tearing into his brain. A smell of burnt flesh wafted around the room as the interrogator persisted, "His name, Philemon?"

"Zikilali," gasped the prisoner.

"The same Zikilali who brought a passbook case to the Supreme Court?"

"Yes, Master."

"Why was he in Durban?"

"He was just telling us about his case."

"And were you trying to organize a strike?"

"No, Master, no."

"What were you meeting him for?"

"Just to hear about his case. Honest."

Erasmus gave a nod and Philemon screamed as his body arched rigidly, dropped and then rapidly lurched again. He heard Van Zyl laughing somewhere in the room.

"Why did you meet him, Philemon?" continued the interrogator.

"Master, please stop, please," begged the prisoner.

"Answer me and we'll stop immediately. Why did you meet him?"

"We were going to make plans to stop people everywhere carrying passbooks. That's all. I'm telling you all I know, Master," he sobbed as his body dropped onto the table again.

The pounding on his knees and feet continued and the flesh became pulpy.

"Michael Zikilali is a member of the communist party. Are you also a member?"

"No, master." He screamed as the power surged through him yet again, and then Van Zyl pressed a dial that cranked his legs up at right angles to his body. He felt a hard, cold object thrust deep into his anus. The Sergeant nodded and a scorching fire exploded in his rectum that ripped deep into his bowels. He screamed in agony.

"I know you're a communist, Philemon. What's your position in the party?" One of the guards handed Erasmus a cigarette and lit it for him. He inhaled deeply on it and then with a swift movement jabbed the lighted end into Philemon's scrotum.

He yelled, "No, I'm not. Michael too, he's not a communist. We're Christians. Please stop, Master."

The questions droned on and on, punctuated with electrical surges, followed by short cessations of current as Philemon's tortured body rose and fell dramatically. As time wore on, the droning voice receded deeper and deeper into the darkness that was taking over his mind, and his body gradually became less aware of the pain until eventually he sank into oblivion.

He was unaware how long he had been comatose, but his first conscious thought on resurfacing was of pain. His genitals felt as if they were raw and on fire. His shoulders and arms felt like they were tearing out of their sockets as he realized that they were stretched above his head with the steel handcuffs biting into his wrists. He struggled to ease the pain by lifting up on his arms, but orders from his brain went unheeded. Raising his head and blinking his eyes to focus, he was able to discern a heavy beam above him and realized that he was hanging suspended from a chain, cast over the beam in his cell. His feet were off the floor but his toes just touched the ground. Stretching, he tried to ease the pain in his upper torso by making. contact with the ground, but the flesh on his feet was swollen and bruised and he cried out in pain. Blood trickled slowly down his arm from the biting cuts in his wrists, and sweat, mixed with tears, dripped from his face. He breathed deeply but the pain in his chest exploded, forcing him to exhale quickly. His throat was parched but there was not even a drop of saliva to slake his thirst. His macabre form dangled like a broken limb on a tree.

Chapter 15

John Msomi lay on his bare mattress and slowly opened his eyes. His throat was dry and his head throbbed intolerably. A dull, persistent knocking, somewhere deep inside his skull, was starting to annoy him and he turned angrily onto his back. The suddenness of the movement stabbed his head like a knife and he put his hands over his eyes, groaning. The knocking persisted and he heard a voice whisper, "John, wake up!"

Slowly he got off his bed and hobbled to the door, clasping his head. "Who's there? What do you want?" he groaned.

"It's me, Simon Gumede. Open up quickly, I must speak to you."

Msomi drew back the latch, blinking at the light and his friend. "Come in, come in. I wish I could say it's good to see you, but I had too much to drink last night. Oh, why do I like beer so much? My brother calls me Chwala, and you can see why."

Simon laughed sympathetically.

"No, don't laugh," replied John. "I know its wrong, but I always drink too much chwala when I've got troubles. Simon, when you get older, find comfort in your friends, not beer." He stumbled back to his bed and lay down again. "Why are you here so early? What time is it?"

"It's time we found Philemon," replied Simon. "Come on, get dressed. We've got a Committee meeting before we go to work. Hurry up. I've already told the attorney that the police have taken Philemon away."

Msomi stood up and as he pulled on his shirt, he asked, "What can the attorney do?"

"He's got friends in high places, maybe even friends in the police force who can help," said Simon.

Not to be outdone, John Msomi straightened up and said, " Well I also know someone who knows people in high places, and he's...." He stopped himself and inwardly cursed his talkativeness.

"He's what?" asked Simon.

"He's um…" John looked around and muttered, "What did I do with my shoes last night?"

Simon pushed them across the floor. "There they are. What are you talking about John? Who do you know and what's he doing?"

"Oh nothing, you know me, I just talk for the sake of talking. Forget it."

"I don't think so. I know you like to talk a lot, but I know you don't lie. So what's going on?" said Simon, grabbing the older man's arm.

"Nothing!" shouted John. "Dammit. You wake me early and then pester me with questions. Now just do me a favor and forget it." He opened his door and let Simon out ahead of him, while searching in his pockets for his key. As he locked the door, he mumbled apologetically, "I'm sorry, Simon. Just forget the whole thing. I'm not very nice first thing in the morning."

Simon felt annoyed with the older man's self loathing. He wondered why Philemon bothered having him on the Committee and supposed it was merely a reward for the hardships he'd suffered, trying to make him feel better. "Philemon's heart is kind, and I suppose it doesn't hurt anyone. I just wish the old guy would shut up though," he thought impatiently.

The two men trudged along the dusty road, and Simon glanced at his companion. He noticed a frown on John's face as he kept looking up at the sky. John Msomi was clearly uneasy. Above them a large hawk was circling and he pointed to it with a grunt. "My ancestors are angry with me. That's their message."

Simon looked up and saw the powerful bird flying around effortlessly and menacingly, but suddenly he saw something else approaching it. "Look carefully, John. See that little bird flying near the hawk. Watch him."

As they spoke, the sparrow began to dive at the larger bird, and within seconds other sparrows joined forces and were swooping and diving at the hawk, which was forced to retreat hastily. Dozens of little dark dots chased the predator, on and on, until it was out of sight.

"So what message do you think your ancestors are giving you?" As John remained silent, Simon continued, "We could learn a lot from those birds. You see what happened there? The sparrow had a big problem he couldn't handle on his own, but with the help of his friends, he had the strength to do so."

John turned to Simon and put his hand on his shoulder. "You're a good friend. But you see my problem is that I've promised someone not to tell you and the Committee something. That troubles me, because I don't like having secrets from my friends."

"This secret," inquired Simon, "does it concern you only, or does it concern someone else?"

"Someone else."

"Can you tell that person?"

"No. That's the trouble. I can't tell him because he's not here. If I could tell him, there wouldn't be a problem!"

They walked in silence as Simon considered what to say. "John," he said finally, "sometimes I think that its good you like to talk so much. There's something going on that concerns Philemon, I can tell. He's our friend too, you know. We all want to help him. So whatever it is, I think you should tell the Committee."

"But I've given my word not to."

"Whom did you give your word to?"

"Toughy Khumalo."

"What?" shrieked Simon. "That man hates Philemon, and Philemon hates him. He calls him the Hyena."

"No, you're wrong. He loves Philemon, he told me. You don't know what you're talking about."

"You're crazy. I saw them fighting in jail when I first met Philemon. It was Toughy that wanted to steal my money. He's bad." Simon stopped and grabbed John by the shoulder. "What've you told him?"

John Msomi hung his head. "I'm not sure. He always buys me drinks and then we talk. I remember that he asks lots of questions when I get drunk, but I don't remember what." He shuffled his feet uncomfortably. "I have to look at some minutes from a meeting for him today, and meet him tonight."

"What minutes?"

"From when Michael came to our meeting. I couldn't remember what happened so he asked me to check."

Simon exhaled loudly. He wanted to shake John Msomi forcibly and tell him what a drunken fool he was, but he knew that would achieve nothing now. What he needed to know was how much damage had been done. "Did Toughy say why he wanted to know this?" he asked, trying not to sound angry.

"Yes, he said his friends who could help us needed to know. Something about convincing the police that Philemon was innocent, I think. Something like that," he nodded. "He's been very nice to me lately, and you know he hasn't been in jail for a long time now. I think maybe he's changed his ways, because he was always in jail for stealing before."

"He's changed his ways alright. He's thought of a different way to get money. He's become an informer. He sells the information you give him to the police. Where do you think he gets the money to buy you all these drinks, Chwala? You can thank the Police for that!" As he was speaking Simon regretted his words, but his anger was so great that he couldn't stop himself. "I'd like to kill that Hyena, slowly and very painfully. We could make a nice necklace for him out of one of these old car tires," he said, kicking at some of the refuse lying at the side of the dirt road, "add a little petrol and a match, and send him straight to hell where he belongs. How could you be so bloody stupid?"

John Msomi was weeping. "I'm so ashamed. My mother is crying in her grave. Simon, I'm sorry."

"It's Philemon you need to say sorry to." The young man suddenly felt very old and wise. He had seen one man's weakness play into the hands of another's greed. He had seen evil at work, corrupting and destroying good. Life was not simple as he had once believed, and those who didn't use their wits, didn't survive. He stared at his tearful companion and saw his guilty anguish, but couldn't forgive him. "Can you think of anything else you've told him? Think, John. We need to tell the attorney everything we can."

"I told him about Philemon going overseas in June. I couldn't remember where he went, but I told him that Philemon was away for two months." John blew his nose loudly, then put his head in his hands and sobbed.

Chapter 16

Captain Du Toit sat at his desk listening to tape recordings from Alan Griffin's office and home. He knew he would hear his daughter's voice on them, but it was still a shock when he did so. He listened as she told her lover of the fight with her father, replaying that section obsessively, until he knew it by heart. He reddened as he heard Alan say, "thank you for loving me so much," and then there were moans and gasps that left him in no doubt about what was happening.

"Dammit!" he thundered, bringing a fist down heavily on his desk as he switched off the tape.

His door immediately opened and the Sergeant's head appeared. "Did you call me, sir?"

"I said dammit. Does that sound like your name? Get the hell out of here." He stormed across to his door and kicked it shut with a shuddering jolt. "You bastard. I'll break your bloody ear off your head if you try listening through the keyhole again."

He marched to his desk and angrily erased that section of the tape, but not from his mind. The humiliation was crippling that his daughter would run from him to the arms of an English liberal, and then share his bed with him. He slammed both fists down as Alan's words echoed in his brain: "If he's got any guts he'll change his views."

"The bastard is so bloody full of shit. Who does he think he is?" he grunted. "Does he know how much guts it takes to do my job while he plays around with some fancy words? But he's right about one thing; my daughter does have guts. Nobody's ever spoken to me like that before. She's got a mind of her own."

He paled suddenly, realizing that he had tampered with evidence by deleting a small portion of the tape. "There's such trouble in America now over this sort of thing," he thought anxiously, cursing his impulsive act. "Agh, this is South Africa, not America. It's my business, not anybody else's. That's all I have to say and I'm the boss."

Chapter 17

The Legal Group was gathered in Alan Griffin's office and the atmosphere was tense. The air-conditioning in the building had been switched off at 5:45 p.m. and as the temperature rose, so did their tempers. It was now 7:30 p.m. and they were still trying to plan their strategy for Philemon's release.

"I say we have a showdown with Captain Du Toit. We demand to know exactly where Philemon is being held and why," shouted Al.

"Oh don't be bloody stupid," countered Angus. "What's he going to say? 'Alan, just because you're going to marry my daughter, I'll tell you, but don't tell anyone else!' Be realistic."

Alan jumped up and banged a fist on his desk. "Give me a better idea. All you do is say what we shouldn't do. I haven't heard any ideas about what we should do. So come on, let's hear it. Let's have your ideas."

"Dammit, I don't have any, but that doesn't mean that I must agree with any old stupid bullshit from you."

"Whoa! Hold it gentlemen. This is getting us nowhere fast," said Dave, placing himself squarely between the two. "Let's just cool tempers down and try to be rational." He watched quietly as Al and

Angus returned to their seats, glowering. Everyone else looked relieved to have the situation diffused and the group relaxed visibly. "What I'm thinking," Dave continued, "is that we have two options. Firstly, as Philemon has been in custody for such a long period, we could apply to the court for a writ of habeas corpus. We have sufficient evidence to establish our case, but the problem is that the Security Police merely have to answer the writ by saying that Philemon has been detained in terms of the Terrorism Act, in which case we're out of court."

He looked at them all over the top of his glasses and continued. "The second possibility, and the one I prefer, is that we talk to Captain Du Toit, as Al suggested, but not with a showdown. That will antagonize him and achieve nothing. I think we must try for a deal. We approach him formally in our capacity as Philemon's legal representatives. He might at least start to talk to us, and the more he talks the more information we have if we're forced to air this incident in the national press."

"I don't particularly like your idea," said John Ngcobo calmly, "but I don't see that we have any other openings. He's our only option."

"That's the way I see it too," agreed Pat Moodley, standing and stretching. "We have very few cards to play, I'm afraid. All we know is that this guy's been taken away by the police, and Du Toit seems the obvious starting point, given his connection to Al and the fact that he's the top of the tree. Let's try and approach him tactfully, and perhaps for that reason it would be better if John and I don't go. The big white chief would find it unacceptable to have two black men approaching him, don't you think?"

"It wouldn't soften his heart to our cause," agreed Dave, "and I don't think Angus and Al have the right chemistry together at the moment. So, I think that leaves me to go with one of you," he said, pushing his glasses up his nose and peering at his two white colleagues.

Angus grunted, "Go with Al. He already knows the bastard."

"Let's go then, Dave, and get it over with. I don't know which is worse, to have me there or not. It's anyone's guess." Al grabbed his jacket from the back of his chair and bolted towards the door.

"Just stay controlled, Al. We achieve nothing if you lose your temper," remonstrated Dave.

They were tense as they drove to the Du Toit's home and neither man spoke. As he glanced in the rear-view mirror, Al noticed a set of lights that seemed to be following them at a distance, one headlamp slightly dimmer than the other. He frowned and bit his bottom lip, trying to decide if he was imagining things. On an impulse, he shouted, "Hold tight!" to Dave, and swiftly swung his Mercedes around a tight corner to take a little used short cut. The lights followed.

They soon pulled up outside their destination and as they were locking the car, Al saw a car stop a little distance down the road and switch off its uneven lights. It was too dark to see anything more and he was tempted to walk towards it to get the license plate number, but he was more anxious to get on with this meeting. His heart was pounding in his chest as they rang the doorbell and he took deep breaths to calm himself.

The door was opened a few inches by the Captain himself. "Oh, it's you. What do you want?" he said curtly, when he saw Al.

Al gritted his teeth, reminding himself to stay calm. "Sir, this is my colleague, David Marais. Could we speak to you for a moment please?"

Du Toit rubbed his chin with his fingers, turning down the corners of his mouth with displeasure. He felt an urge to punch Alan's nose as he recollected the taped conversations he'd heard between this man and his daughter. With great difficulty he restrained himself, knowing any such action would push Helena further away. He sniffed and grunted, "Marais, hey. Well, I suppose you'd better come in. We can't talk here on the doorstep." Reluctantly he opened the door fully and showed them into the front room.

"Sit down," he muttered, gesturing towards two chairs, then removed his newspaper from his own chair and put it on the floor beside him. Slowly he lit his pipe and observed Alan through the smoke. He noticed the pink shirt and bright tie, and the gold chain across the arch of each shoe. "He looks like a gigolo," he thought to himself, "Wouldn't be surprised if he wears a bloody necklace. He needs a good haircut too. But this friend of his is a miserable apology for a man. At least Griffin has a bit of muscle on him and if he weren't wearing fancy dress he'd look okay. Only his mother could love the other one though." He sucked his pipe and said, "Well, what do you want?"

"Sir," began David respectfully, "we'd like to speak to you about Philemon Dlamini, a client of ours."

"What about him?"

"We know you have him in custody, sir, and we'd like to know where he's being held."

"I'm not at liberty to discuss this with you," replied the Captain, slowly exhaling and watching the smoke hang lazily above his head.

"What harm can it do to tell us that?" demanded Al, feeling anger welling up inside him.

"It has nothing to do with you. I don't give out information to somebody just because they ask for it! I don't give information to anybody, end of story."

As Al opened his mouth to respond, Dave quickly restrained him by answering first. "Captain, we are here in our professional capacities as Philemon's duly appointed attorneys. That gives us authority to ask his whereabouts."

"It does, does it?" replied the older man unruffled. "Well, I regret to inform you that the state doesn't give me the authority to discuss the case with you. Furthermore, this is my home, not my office. I never bring work home."

Al took a deep breath and plunged in again. "You know Sir, you have the most powerful police force backing you, and yet you are not prepared to even discuss the matter with two attorneys. I think you're scared that you don't have a case."

"Now I've heard everything," the Captain snorted with laughter. "You think I'm scared! I'm trying to remember the last time I felt scared and I can't think of it. Must've been a long time ago - probably before you were born."

Dave noted the glint in the Captain's eyes and knew that they'd ruffled his composure. "I can understand that, sir," he added quickly, "especially with the backing you have. That's why we can't understand your reluctance to give us some information. Philemon's family would really appreciate knowing that he's safe."

"He's safe. I'll tell you that much. He's safe where you can't touch him, not even with a court order. He's been detained in terms of Section Six of the Terrorism Act," he finished triumphantly.

Al and Dave glanced at each other as the Captain rocked in his chair with a look of satisfaction. "How long do you intend holding him?" asked Dave.

"As long as it takes. When we have all the information we require, we'll charge him in court, or release him. You know that."

Al tapped his foot impatiently. "Are you torturing him?"

"I'd like you to leave now. I've had enough of your nonsense. You know very well this is a civilized country and we don't use such methods." He got up and opened the door for them to leave.

Al felt frustrated by the smug self-righteousness of his future father-in-law. He wanted to inflict pain and get a reaction from him. As he stood up to leave he said, "By the way, Helen and I have decided to get married next month. We'll send you some pictures." He smiled as he saw the old man pale and grasp the door handle tightly. He added as an afterthought, "Just thought I'd let you know before your bully-boys report back to you about it. Their trailing methods are a bit obvious you know."

The two attorneys walked out leaving a shaken father staring at the door after he'd slammed it shut.

"When was this decision made?" asked Dave in amazement.

"About ten seconds ago," laughed Al. "Best decision I've made in a long time. Hope H.A. agrees because there's really no point in waiting with things as they are. Did you see the look on his face? Man, that felt good. Get him where it hurts most. And at least we know what's cooking with Philemon, not that it helps too much."

****

In another part of town, on the cold concrete floor of the interrogation room, Philemon sat with his hands manacled behind his back, and his feet tied together. He watched the final bucket of ice-cold water being poured into the concrete bath by two guards, while Sergeant Erasmus stood to one side, gazing impassively, and Warder Van Zyl stood at the foot of the bath, his eyes bright with anticipation. As they finished pouring the water, the two guards stripped to their underwear. Erasmus went up to the black man and squatted on his haunches next to him.

"This is going to be unpleasant. But you can stop it anytime you want if you decide to talk. Just call out when you come up for air, and we'll rest and listen to you. You understand?"

A hook attached to a pulley on the ceiling was clipped to his handcuffs, and then Philemon was lifted by machine from the floor. The pulley system creaked and shuddered as it moved its victim to hang over the bath, at which point it lowered him into the water. The shock of the cold shot through his body but then he realized that the pain in his swollen feet and knees was decreasing as they numbed to the cold. It was a relief. He felt too tired to struggle, even when he was immersed up to his neck. It was then he resolved not to struggle again. They could kill him if they chose, and if they didn't, he would bide his time and kill one of them. That would get him into court and he would tell his story to the world.

Suddenly the mechanical gratings were interrupted by a loud, human scream, "Now." The two guards pounced on top of Philemon and pushed him completely under the water.

Resisting the basic desire to fight back, Philemon kept his body completely limp. This caused confusion and his captors gazed at each other in consternation. Erasmus called, "Bring him up." Water splashed all over the room and the men jumped back expecting violence, but still Philemon lay quietly, gasping for air. Walking to the edge of the bath, Erasmus threatened, "Listen, my boy, this is

116

your last chance to talk. Next time we push your head under, we won't let it come up again."

Philemon worked up as much thick mucous as he could in his mouth, and turning his head, spat forcibly in the Sergeant's face. Erasmus washed his face in the cold water and looked coldly at the prisoner. "You've done that once too often." He walked away and nodded at Van Zyl.

"Now!" The word was screamed again and once more Philemon was forcibly plunged underwater by the two guards. Slowly he exhaled the air in his lungs and lay limply under the surface of the water. Feeling his eyes were about to pop out of his head and his chest was about to burst, he gulped for air uncontrollably, and immediately choked. As the cold water entered his lungs he felt himself float blissfully away in a gray mist.

****

Simon Gumede had just left a committee meeting and walked dejectedly into the dark night. He was becoming increasingly disillusioned with the efforts they were making, as they never brought any results. Philemon was still detained and John Msomi was an idiot. The Hyena was every bit as bad as he'd ever thought he was, and the white attorneys hadn't been able to trace Philemon.

It was a summer night, but there were still fires burning inside many houses. They gave light long after the food had been cooked, and everybody felt much safer when they could see. There was a muted murmur of voices behind each door, but nobody came out in the street.

"They think they're safe inside there," mused Simon, "but none of us are safe anywhere. They took Philemon right out of his room. We're defenseless." He angrily kicked some dirt. "It's bad when you don't feel safe in the street, because someone might attack you, but you can't feel safe in your room because the police can take you away. That story I told John Msomi the other day," he thought to himself, "the answer to all this is in that story. The little birds joined together to chase the powerful bird away. He was stronger but they had the numbers to overcome his size."

He stopped still, staring into the night as if he saw something in the darkness. "I know you don't think it's right, Philemon," he · whispered apologetically, "but it's not right what they've done to you. Nothing they do is right. What choice do they leave us? How else can we change anything?" His soft words in the night absolved all guilt that had confused him for days. "I am ready for Sipu and Joe now."

He knew they would approach him again soon, and that when they did, he would have to go away and learn how to be a soldier. He wondered where he would be sent and hoped it would be somewhere near his home in Northern Natal. He couldn't know that when they did come for him, he would be sent far away to a strange, cold land of ice and snow, where men spoke a language he'd never heard before.

Chapter 18

Philemon was dragged back to his cell, semi-conscious and gasping for breath. The rope was once again passed through his arms and he was lifted into the air, to hang once more from the ceiling by his still manacled hands. His body was covered with goose pimples and he shivered uncontrollably. Nausea flowed through him and he heaved, but only a dry, grating sound came from his burning throat. His body ached and his hands bled from the metal biting into his skin. He groaned out loud and the sound of his own voice startled him into full wakefulness. Remembering his resolve, his eyes brightened. "Yes, one of them will die."

As if on cue, he heard the bolt of his cell door being drawn back. He watched, tense and alert, to see Van Zyl enter and sneer at him. "Ja kaffir," the Warder barked, "not looking so good, are you." Slowly he drew a knife out of his pocket and flicked open the blade, holding it up to the light so that it glinted in Philemon's eyes. "Ja, today I'm going to ask the questions, and you will give me the answers I want. If you don't, kaffir, I'm going to do some plastic surgery on your balls. It'll be a shame if you can't keep your wife happy any more."

He laughed coarsely and turned the blade a few times. Philemon watched like a leopard, ready to spring.

"Ja, but maybe I can keep her happy for you hey! I've often wondered what a bit of chocolate would be like." He smirked and came closer. "I think I'll..."

He never finished the sentence. Philemon pulled himself up on the rope with his hands and in a flash swung himself forward, kicking out with his legs. One foot caught the Warder just above his heart, and the other caught the wrist of the hand holding the knife. Van Zyl flew across the cell, falling in a crumpled heap at the door. Nobody would ever be certain whether he fell on the knife, or whether the force of the kick made him stab himself before he fell.

****

Alan was working late at his desk when the phone rang and a familiar voice said, "Griffin, this is Captain Du Toit here. Are you still acting for Philemon Dlamini?"

"Of course I am," answered Al brusquely.

"Well if you want to see him, take down this address. Go there at once and I'll arrange for you to get access to him."

Al grabbed a pencil and said, "Okay, what's the address?" He copied it down and said, "Mind if I bring someone with me?" Something seemed amiss.

"Who?"

"David Marais."

"Good idea. Your client is in big trouble."

"What do you mean? He's been locked up."

"Hasn't stopped him getting into trouble. We're looking at attempted murder, maybe even murder by now," snapped Du Toit and the line went dead.

The address was in a less affluent part of town and appeared to be a block of five or six apartments, two storeys high. It was well-lit and set back about ten yards from the road. Alongside the sidewalk was a lawn with a few shrubs, surrounded by a four-foot wall with a steel gate. The lawn was also in bright light, quite out of keeping with the dingy neighborhood. Al noticed all this as he parked his car and opened the gate with Dave. As they walked towards the building, a figure suddenly jumped up from behind a shrub to challenge them.

"What do you want?"

"We've come to see a friend," replied Dave.

"Your friend's not here." The figure blocked their way on the path.

"And how the hell do you know that? You don't even know who my friend is," demanded Al, advancing on the figure. "Get out my way."

"Bliksem," the stranger cursed, "You just try and get past me and see what happens to you."

Without hesitation, Al swung his left fist at the stranger's jaw. The man swayed backwards from the blow and tried to swing a punch at Al as he righted himself, but the attorney ducked and kicked his assailant's legs from beneath him, shouting, " I said get out of my bloody way."

"What's going on here?" called a voice from the building. Al looked up to see Captain Du Toit at the door.

"That's a good question," retorted Al, with his arms still raised aggressively. "Maybe you'd like to explain to us what's going on. How many bastards have you got hiding in the bushes? Oh and look, here comes another one in the gate. I'll get him Dave, you watch this freak."

"It's okay," soothed the Captain, "this was a mistake. Nobody's trying to attack you, and I suggest you don't attack my staff in future. Come inside quickly. That's Sergeant Erasmus behind you. Come along Sergeant."

The Captain turned on his heel and marched back through the door, followed angrily by Al, Dave and the Sergeant. He led them into a reception room with four chairs in it. "Go and tell them to bring Philemon here," ordered the Captain, and Erasmus dutifully left the room. "I'll give you fifteen minutes in here with him, that's all."

"What's he been charged with?" inquired Dave.

"Attempted murder at this stage. He stabbed a warder. If the man dies, it becomes a murder charge. He could swing for this."

Al looked at him with disbelief. "He attempted to murder a warder while in custody. Is that what you're telling me?"

"That's correct. It was a vicious attack. Here's your client now," he said, opening the door, "I'll leave you in here to question him." The Captain disdainfully watched the prisoner shuffle into the room, and then left, closing the door after himself.

Al jumped up and grabbed Philemon's hand, which was swathed in bandages. He saw the painful reaction on the man's face and gently let go his grip. "What have they done to you?" he gasped. "Here, sit down and tell us what's happened."

"It's been hard," murmured Philemon, slowly slumping into a chair. "You can't believe all that they have done." His voice started to fade and his hands shook.

"What's this about attempted murder?"

"I only wish I'd killed him. He was coming at me with a knife while I was hanging tied up in the air. He said he was going to cut my balls off. I was weak, but I kicked as hard as I could and he knifed himself instead. Maybe there's still a God up there after all. I thought He'd deserted me or died or something."

Alan pulled his chair closer and said gently, "What all did they do to you?"

Philemon shook his head and tears poured unashamedly down his face. He pulled up his trouser legs to reveal his grossly swollen ankles and knees. "They beat me. They put electricity into me - even in places you can't believe. They tried to drown me. They fired guns past my head. They did everything except kill me. They locked me up in a cell and tied me up, leaving me hanging from the roof." At this point he was seized with a painful coughing fit. "They gave me hardly any food or water," he sobbed between coughs.

The room was silent as the two attorneys stared and tried to understand what they had just heard. They looked at one another stunned. Suddenly Al jumped up and pulled open the door, shouting, "Captain, please come here at once."

Du Toit entered the room and looked with distaste at Philemon. "What lies have you been telling?"

"Captain, you know I would rather not speak at all than tell a lie," the prisoner said scornfully.

"Captain," demanded Al, walking around to confront the policeman, "I want this man examined by a doctor immediately."

"He has already been examined by a doctor," was the nonchalant reply.

Turning to Philemon, Al inquired, "Is this true?"

"Yes. But that was days ago. I've had more injuries since then," he said, indicating his hands and legs. "Lots more."

"Okay, Captain," said Al menacingly, "let's cut the crap here. This man is injured and needs a doctor."

"He fell down a flight of stairs," stated Du Toit.

"They always do, don't they! We'll argue about that later. Right now, we need a doctor immediately."

Du Toit was undecided. He glared at Al, who took a step towards him. "Is there something you don't understand? Let me repeat it for you, slowly. Get a doctor to my client immediately."

The Captain went to the door and called out, "Erasmus, get Dr. Meyer here."

"He's off duty tonight, Sir," came the reply.

"Find him and get him here immediately. That's an order!"

Du Toit turned to face the attorneys again. "Listen here," he began, "I'm going to warn you right now that if you step out of line, just one little step, your futures as attorneys will be up to shit. That goes for both of you. You'd better play by the book or I'll throw the bloody book at you. Do you hear?"

Dave put a restraining arm on Al. "Captain," he replied, "We don't need your advice. We know what we're doing."

Al was not easily restrained. He swallowed hard, thrust Dave's arm aside and strode up to Du Toit. "You can take your advice and stick it up your arse with some electricity to help it on its way. And you might want to refresh yourself on the Geneva Convention while you're about it."

As the Captain glared at Al, his face turned red with fury. He turned and strode out of the room, cursing under his breath. The two attorneys looked at the prisoner sitting hunched on the chair. He was smiling weakly. "You don't know how good it is to see you again," he sighed deeply, and then doubled up with the pain in his ribs.

Chapter 19

Helen awoke and sat up as Mary handed her a cup of coffee. "Special room service for you today. Rise and shine, lady, this is the first day of the rest of your life," Mary greeted her cheerfully. "I'm here to get you up and looking beautiful. You're not allowed to see Al until you walk into the church." She sat down on the bed next to her and added, "How does it feel to be a bride?"

Helen sniffed and stared into her coffee. Nothing seemed quite real to her and it certainly seemed very strange to think that this was her wedding day. Everything had been so rushed and she still wasn't sure why she'd agreed to bring the date forward so drastically. When she considered her actions, she thought they were prompted by anger and seemed like a way of getting back at her father, which made her feel petty and childish. She turned and looked at Mary, saying, "If you really want to know, it feels awful. I feel like a five year old, but I want my mother."

"Oh for God's sake, H.A. If you want your mother, go and pick up the phone and call her. You're being as stubborn as your father and you're hurting your mother as well as yourself. Don't be such an idiot," Mary said with exasperation.

Tears welled up in Helen's eyes. "Al's Mom has been very kind, but I really miss my Ma," she said, almost to herself. Alan's mother had been convinced that H.A. was pregnant and was fretting over what her friends would think. "Such indecent haste!" she had complained. "I don't know how to explain it in my Christmas cards. I'm sure all my friends were expecting a big wedding at the Johannesburg Country Club when the time came. What am I going to say?"

"How about saying 'Happy Christmas!' For God's sake, Mother, that's exactly why we want to do it this way. We don't want all your friends gaping at us. They couldn't give a rat's arse anyway; they just want a free meal and champagne. Now if you don't want to come and celebrate with us, just say so," Alan had replied with his usual fire. "I don't think Helen's parents will be there either."

"Good God. Why ever not? I wasn't looking forward to meeting them, but this is unthinkable."

"Seems like you aren't the only parents not thrilled with the match."

"How dare they!" Hilda responded. "How dare they! Do they even begin to understand what a catch you are for their daughter?"

Alan roared with laughter and said, "It would seem that they don't. There's no accounting for taste, is there."

Hilda had been very sympathetic after that exchange, taking pity on H.A. and moving happily into the maternal role. She had helped choose the dress, offered the veil from her own wedding, and had organized the wedding to take place in St. James' Church, not a registry office. "Too cold and impersonal," she had insisted. Helen and Al had been happy to let her take charge, but refused any reception at all, compromising with a small lunch party at the Edward Hotel.

As Helen finished her coffee she turned to Mary, who was still sitting on the bed watching her friend wrestle with herself. "You're right. I've got to be bigger than this," she said. "Just because Pa's a jerk, I don't have to be one too." She grabbed the phone and called her mother before she lost the resolve.

"Ma," she began, "I don't know how to tell you this, but I've kind of made a mess of things."

"What's happened Helena, where have you been?" Engela replied.

"Didn't Dad tell you that he threw me out?"

There was a stunned silence on the other end. "I'm not phoning about that, Ma. I'm phoning to tell you that I'm getting married today and I really want you and Dad to be there. Please Ma. I know I should've told you before, but I was just so mad with Pa that I couldn't. But now the day has come and I want you to be there, Ma. I'm sorry, please come, please." There was still silence on the other end. "Ma, are you there?"

"Yes Helena, I'm here. I'm trying to take all this in. I don't really understand."

"I know. I've been a fool."

"Marriage is forever, Helena. It's not something you do to spite your father."

"I don't have any doubts about Al, Ma - trust me. But I feel miserable because I'm not sharing my wedding day with you. I'm sorry that we planned it without you, but can we at least *celebrate* with you? I don't know if I'll feel properly married if you're not there."

"I'll speak to your father. This is a bit of a shock. Tell me when and where."

"Eleven o'clock at St. James' Anglican Church in Venice Road. Please come."

"I'll speak to your father. I hope everything goes well for you both. Goodbye." There was a click and then the line went dead.

H.A. felt tears spring to her eyes as she replaced the phone, and said a silent prayer for forgiveness, knowing the hurt she'd heard in her mother's voice. She was still standing there when the phone rang. As she picked it up she heard a sniff and her mother's gentle voice saying, "Helena?"

"Yes, Ma," she responded eagerly.

"I just want to give you my blessing, my darling. I pray that God will bring you much happiness and joy with this man that you love so much. God bless you both."

Mrs. Du Toit promptly set out on an urgent mission to get to her daughter's wedding. First stop was her husband, whose fury was like an explosion of a septic boil. "Never, never will I have anything to do with her again, and neither will you. Do you understand?"

"You can't do that Fanie. If you choose to cut her out of your life that's your business, but you can't make me do that too. She's my daughter," Engela had bravely countered. "I don't think you should behave like that, and I don't think you should tell me what to do."

"Dammit. What is happening here? No wonder your daughter doesn't listen to me. Why should she when her mother doesn't either? My final word is that I don't want anything more to do with her and I forbid you to go to this wedding. And it's in an Anglican Church!" He shuddered. "That's the last straw. If you set foot in that church Engela, you'll find me moving into the spare bedroom."

"Don't tempt me," she muttered under her breath.

"What did you say?" he demanded.

"I said you're a fool. You let your stupid pride get in the way and now you will lose a daughter," she replied, staring straight up into his face. "If we go today to her wedding, everything will eventually come right. She's going to marry this man; we can't change that. We have to learn to like him. If we don't go today, we make the situation worse and we may never heal all this pain. It'll get bigger and bigger. We'll all be living with regrets, just because of your stupid pride. What will it take then to heal all this?"

"I'm telling you once and for all, I wouldn't cross the street to help her if she fell down. Not until she apologizes and behaves honorably. She's been living in sin. She's a disgrace. You can talk until you're blue in the face, but nothing will change my mind."

"When she's married she won't be living in sin. Have you thought about that? God gave you a daughter and it's not for you to cast her aside, you stupid man."

"Engela, that's enough. My mind is made up."

She turned on her heel and left his office. Looking at her watch, she saw that it was already 10:15 a.m. There would be no time to change her clothes but if she caught a bus into town immediately, she could find out at the terminal how to get to Venice Road. She felt agitated as she sat down on the bus and closed her eyes to try composing her thoughts. It was such a long time since she'd caught the bus downtown that she'd quite forgotten how long it took to reach the terminal. She knew she was running out of time and looked around desperately for a taxi, but they all appeared to be for blacks only. She looked at her watch - it was 10:55am. Finally she asked a bus driver on a whites only bus, how she could get to Venice Road.

"That's in Morningside, isn't it? You'll have to go up Pine Street and catch a Number 36 bus at the stop outside Payne Brothers. Here, stay on this bus and I'll let you off up there. I leave in three minutes - have you there in another ten. You might just make the 11:20 bus. Otherwise it'll be a long wait because there aren't many buses on Saturdays."

Tears of frustration sprang to her eyes as she took a seat and tried to contain herself. Here she was just sitting, waiting, and her daughter would be walking up the aisle any minute. She wanted to scream, but controlled herself with difficulty. She realized with a sudden shake of her head, that she hadn't given a thought to her husband's admonitions. She searched for a tissue in her bag and blew her nose softly.

The Number 36 bus dropped her off in Essenwood Road, near the corner of Venice, and then a good three blocks to St. James' according to the bus driver. "You can do it in five minutes if you hurry." Her watch showed that it was now 11:45 a.m. She was exhausted, but adrenalin gave her the energy to keep going at a pace. Her heart was racing and sweat was beginning to pour from her brow as she struggled up steep Essenwood Road. She could see the corner twenty yards ahead and then it would be flat, she consoled herself. Gasping for breath she leaned against a tree to steady herself for a moment. The pounding in her chest was visible and she feared that she might have a heart attack. "Not now, dear God, please give me strength to get there in time. I'm almost there."

Her throat was dry and her head pounded as she reached the corner and turned into Venice Road. There was St. James' Church.

"If I'm quick, I might make it in time for some of the ceremony. Maybe they started late."

She broke into an excited run, straining to see if the cars outside the church had anybody in them. Running all the while and peering ahead, she heard the bells start to peal and then, as the church doors opened, she saw the bride and groom emerge. She gasped and with that felt herself sprawl to the ground, her ankle twisting underneath her.

"No," she cried in agony, with pain shooting through her foot.

Keeping her eyes on her daughter, she tried to pull herself up, but when she tried to do so, she couldn't put any weight on her left foot. She was loathe to take her eyes off Helena, but glimpsed down to see what had happened. There was blood pouring from both her knees and hands and suddenly she was overcome with frustration. She couldn't embarrass her daughter appearing like this at her wedding, even if she were able to hop all the way across the street and get there in time. After all this, to be so near and yet out of reach, was hard to bear. She realized that she was swimming in perspiration, and that her hair had come undone, hanging in straggles about her face. Her old dress that she'd been wearing when she'd left home in such haste, was now covered in blood and dirt after her fall. It would never do to be seen like this at her daughter's wedding. Stoically she hopped to lean against a tree and hide in its shade, for now she was desperate not to be seen.

"Fanie would say I deserve what I got. If only he weren't so difficult and stubborn, he could have driven us here and none of this would have happened. If only he could have seen what a beautiful bride our Helena made," she said to herself. Tears streamed down her face as she watched her daughter and new son-in-law smiling for the photographer, with an older man and woman standing on either side of them. She buried her head in her hands and sobbed.

Helen had been hopeful that her mother, at least, would be in the church. She felt guilty as she walked up the aisle on Dave's arm instead of her father's, and looked around the small congregation in anticipation of seeing their faces watching her. She saw Mary smiling brightly but felt a stab of disappointment that her parents weren't there. She chided herself for not calling earlier, but straightened and smiled bravely, remembering her mother's blessing. "I know she's thinking of me, and she wants me to be happy. Now this is my wedding day and I'll concentrate on the man I'm about to marry." She looked at him standing tall and proud, waiting for her, and smiled.

The ceremony was short but beautiful and she laughed happily as they walked out of the church, arm in arm, into the bright sunshine. "Smile, Mrs. Griffin," the waiting photographer said, and it was easy to oblige. He took pictures of the couple and then called for some shots with the parents. As the group arranged themselves, she felt herself fighting back an urge to cry again as a sense of loss gripped her. The group wouldn't be complete.

For an instant as they drove away, she thought she saw her mother on the other side of the road, but it was very shady and she couldn't be sure. When she looked again, there was nothing.

Chapter 20

Machines beeped eerily at regular intervals and intravenous apparatus dripped clear liquids into the inert mass of flesh that had once been the arm of the law. Warder Van Zyl breathed by himself, but all other bodily functions required assistance. He occasionally opened his eyes as he heard the squeak of nurses' shoes on the sterile, linoleum floor, or when he heard Mrs. Van Zyl weeping and blowing her nose loudly at his bedside. For a moment he would register her presence with a small nod that started a ripple through his limp jowls, before he drifted back into unconsciousness.

Days turned into endless weeks as he battled for his life at Entabeni Hospital's Intensive Care Unit. His left lung had collapsed from the knife wound, and he had lost nearly two pints of blood. Emergency procedures had pulled him back from certain death, but the Grim Reaper still hovered closely, hoping the vigilant medical team would falter on their watch.

However at King Edward VIIIth Hospital for Blacks, Philemon gained strength in the closely policed prison ward. He was given nutritious, regular meals and careful medical treatment, and after a week his body began to feel well again. The swollen flesh on his feet and knees gradually eased, and the wounds on his wrists mended. His abdomen still ached from the abuse it had suffered, but gradually, with a decent diet and liquid, his bodily functions painfully resumed their normal activity. The welts and bruises on his body faded too, and after a month he once more looked a fine, strong Zulu man - a man who could plausibly commit murder.

Alan Griffin and David Marais had tried hard to bring Philemon's case to court as soon as possible, but it was remanded until after the Christmas recess.

The Christmas season was not uniformly filled with goodwill towards man. While carefree holidaymakers basked in summer sunshine on the beaches, or flocked to Kingsmead to watch Currie Cup Cricket with a great sense of bonhomie, Al and David worked methodically, interviewing witnesses, studying medical reports on both Van Zyl and Philemon, discussing these with doctors, and studying law reports. They made sure that Philemon's injuries were well documented and photographed, knowing that the Prosecution would never be ready for trial while any evidence of mistreatment was visible on the prisoner.

****

H.A. woke up very early crying that Christmas morning. Alan's arms were wrapped protectively around her in his sleep, and she squeezed her eyes to try and stop her tears. Waking or sleeping these days, sadness and guilt gnawed its way into her brain. It was Christmas and she hadn't seen her parents, but she couldn't reconcile herself to her father's job and his attitude towards Alan. She was in shock discovering that her father was connected to the brutality meted out to Philemon and was repulsed by the thought of it. She felt more sadness and guilt thinking about her wedding; ashamed of the hurt she'd caused her mother. She told herself that it was the marriage and not the wedding that mattered; that her husband was a remarkable man and that's all that counted, but her happiness was marred by her guilt and emptiness. She tried to conceal it from Al, who was enveloped in preparations for this upcoming trial which she knew would involve her father. Sleep gave no reprieve from her corrosive worries.

She slipped out of bed and went to the telephone, staring at it for some time. Finally she picked it up and dialed her parents' number, willing her mother to answer. The phone rang interminably and as she was about to replace the receiver she heard it being picked up. Her heart was in her mouth as she heard her mother answer in a breathless voice, "Good morning, Engela Du Toit speaking."

Helena burst into tears that she tried to choke. She heard her mother repeat, "Hello, Engela Du Toit here. Can I help you?"

"Mom, it's me," H.A. sobbed, "I just phoned to say I love you, and Happy Christmas."

"Helena, I knew you'd phone. Thank you, thank you my angel. Will you come to Church with us today?"

"I don't know, Ma. I can't face Pa."

"It's Christmas, Helena. You can't wish me a happy Christmas and really mean it if you do this to me."

"He told me to get out until I mend my ways. That's why I left."

Engela sighed and frowned. "I don't know what's going on between you and your father, but I am also your parent. You will always be my daughter and I will always love you, no matter what. I'll be waiting for you whenever you're ready to come back to me."

"I love you so much, Ma. I'm sorry that all this is hurting you. I just don't know what to do. Please believe in me."

"I've never stopped doing that and I never will. God bless you, my angel, you'll work it out, whatever it is. You'll always know where you can find me."

In the background Helena heard a door slam and then her father's voice calling. "I'd better let you go, Ma," she said quickly, "I'll call you again."

Fanie and Engela sat silently together on Christmas morning. Engela said nothing about the phone call. They waited until the last minute before going to church, hoping that their daughter would appear at their sides. Engela prayed fervently on her knees for peace in her home. Fanie stared at the altar, and listened to the sermon that brought him no peace of mind. He felt betrayed by his daughter and angry that God could let that happen to him when he had been such a good father. "You should've had a daughter, God," he thought wryly. "It was easy for you to be a Father, because you had such a perfect Son. But I don't know what to do anymore."

Mrs. Van Zyl's prayers were answered that Christmas morning when her husband finally opened his eyes and kept them open. He lifted his arm weakly and touched her hand, which caused her to burst into tears. "Thanks be to God," she yelled, bringing nurses scurrying to her husband's bedside. The Grim Reaper sighed and departed, and Warder Van Zyl was taken off the critical list and out of Intensive Care.

Philemon was taken out of hospital and returned to prison on Christmas Eve. It was not his old cell though, and it didn't appear to be the same prison. He could see other inmates crowded in cells around him as he was marched along a corridor. There was noisy shouting from both prisoners and police and he felt a rush of relief to see so many of his own people again - and to hear Zulu voices and to feel part of the human race. He smiled and shouted greetings to them in response to their calls of sympathy and encouragement. As he was pushed into a solitary cell, far away from the other prisoners, he felt his skin go cold with emotion when they began singing "Nkosi Sikelela Afrika," and then as one body they broke into "Silent Night," with voices soaring. He listened to their harmony in the distance and found himself singing quietly with them. He hadn't even realized, until now, that it was Christmas and he slowly knelt down on his tender knees to pray for his wife and child. "Please protect them God. Please relieve our suffering, and please forgive me for what I did. What else could I do? Please don't let hate kill this land. God help Africa."

In the distance he heard the cathedral bells pealing and tears welled in his eyes. Christmas was here and Christians everywhere would be praying for peace and goodwill. Would it ever happen?

Chapter 21

In January, the festive lights in West. Street came down, Christmas trees with aerosol snow were discarded, and as the Christmas season officially came to an end, the courts began their burdensome task once more. Al and Dave sensed that they would be given a court date soon. Philemon was out of hospital now and Warder Van Zyl was recovering, so the charge remained one of attempted murder. They were finally notified that they should appear in court on the twenty-first of January 1974.

The Attorney General himself, Deon Kingsley Q.C., was prosecuting on behalf of the State, and with him was appearing Len de Villiers. They sat close together in deep conversation, reviewing their plan of attack that had been worked out weeks before. Al and Dave sat together at the Bar, neatly setting out law books, medical reports and papers. The tension was electric.

Judge Kenneth Hughes was to preside, an announcement that had been met with approval by both the State and Defense. Judge Hughes was noted for allowing greater latitude in cross-examination of witnesses than some of his colleagues. At exactly ten o'clock, the door of the Judge's Chambers swung open and the court usher emerged, shouting, "Silence in court!"

The packed courtroom rose and comparative silence prevailed, broken only by occasional shuffling of feet and clearing of throats as Mr. Justice Hughes approached the Bench. He regally bowed to the court, and the attorneys at the Bar returned the courtesy. Once the noise of scraping chairs and whispered comments had died down as people re-seated themselves, the Clerk of the Court began the proceedings by rising to face the Judge and intoning, "M'Lord, I call the case of the State versus Philemon Dlamini."

Deon Kingsley took his cue to announce, "M'Lord, may it please you, I appear for the State, assisted by my learned friend, Mr. De Villiers."

As Kingsley sat down, Alan rose and addressed the Judge. "May it please you, M'Lord, I appear for the accused, assisted by Mr. Marais."

The Clerk of the Court now required the accused to stand. Philemon, dressed in gray trousers with a neat jacket and open-necked shirt, slowly rose to his full height.

"Are you Philemon Dlamini?" inquired the Clerk.

"I am."

The Clerk read from a piece of paper. "Philemon Dlamini, the charge against you is one of attempted murder, in that on or about the eighth of November, 1973, and at Durban, you did wrongfully, unlawfully, and maliciously attempt to kill Jacobus Franciscus Van Zyl. How do you plead to this charge?"

Philemon's deep voice resonated loudly through the courtroom, "Not guilty."

"You may be seated Mr. Dlamini," replied the Judge curtly, and then turning to the prosecuting team he added, "Please begin, Mr. Kingsley."

The trial had started.

Senior Prosecution Counsel, Deon Kingsley, rose ponderously to his feet, hooked his thumbs in the pockets of his waistcoat and began to address the court. "M'Lord, this is not a run-of-the-mill charge which the accused faces. We will endeavor to prove that the attempt on the life of Warder Van Zyl was premeditated. We will lead evidence to show that, while in the custody of the Security Police, the accused's conduct was such that the only conclusion the court will be able to reach, was that the accused intended to defy authority and cause as much trouble as possible.

"We will show that while being interrogated, the accused openly defied two of his warders, one of whom was a senior officer. Finally we will show that the accused threatened Warder Van Zyl and we will ask the court to find, as a fact, that from the circumstances of the threat, it was a threat to kill. In all these circumstances we will suggest to the court that we have proved, beyond reasonable doubt, that the accused did wrongfully, unlawfully and maliciously attempt to murder Warder Van Zyl."

As Kingsley sat down, the Judge nodded at Al and said, "Yes, Mr. Griffin?"

Alan arose and as always happened to him when he started to speak, nervousness left him and his concentration was complete. "M'Lord, with your permission, I will reserve the Defense's address until after the State has put forward its case, should it be necessary. At this point I will merely give a brief explanation of the Defense's case so that M'Lord will understand my line when cross-examining witnesses." He looked up at the Judge and then at the Prosecution to receive a response, considering this a shrewd opening as it informed the Judge that he felt the State did not have a strong case.

Deon Kingsley Q.C. shrugged his shoulders nonchalantly as he rose slightly in his chair. "I have no objection to my learned friend's suggestion, M'Lord," he replied, and slumped back into his chair, subtly informing the Judge that the Prosecution was confident with its case. The cut and thrust of battle had started.

"In that case, Mr. Griffin, please proceed," ruled the Judge, as he leaned forward intently and placed his elbows on the Bench.

"M'Lord," Alan began, "the Defense will attempt to disprove the allegations made by my learned friend in his opening address. In fact M'Lord, we will attempt to show that the accused's actions, whilst in the custody of the Security Police, were automatic responses. The accused was so conditioned by what he had experienced whilst in custody, that he was operating on a level of purely reflex actions. We will attempt to show that whilst in custody of the Security Police, my client was viciously and mercilessly tortured."

The public gallery exploded with excited response and journalists scrambled for the door, in search of telephones to inform the world of the Defense allegations. Al sat down as the Judge banged angrily on the Bench, and the Court Usher and policemen demanded silence. At first their efforts were futile, but gradually the room grew silent again and Judge Hughes admonished everyone, "If there is a repetition of this outbreak at any time during this trial, I will clear the public galleries." Then, turning his attention to the journalists near the door where the police had barred their way, he continued, "Ladies and Gentlemen of the Press, you should know better than to behave like this. If you don't show more respect, your privilege of sitting in the Well of the court will be withdrawn." After glaring icily at them as they retreated to their seats, he turned his attention once more to the Prosecution and nodded, "Proceed."

Kingsley rose ponderously again and nodded at Al, acknowledging the impact his adversary had made. "M'Lord, I call my first witness, Captain Du Toit of the Security Police."

The Captain entered through a side door and went into the witness box, where the Clerk of the Court administered the oath. He was watched in the spectator's gallery by Helen, who felt a cold shiver as he promised to tell the truth, the whole truth and nothing but the truth. This was the first time she'd seen him since their argument and she felt a resurgence of turmoil as she looked at him now. In her heart she viewed him to be on trial rather than Philemon. She watched him fumble nervously for his pipe, which he knew he couldn't smoke here, and then clear his throat. She knew all his mannerisms so well, but this case had filled her with horror at the limitless bounds of his cruelty. Nothing he believed in could justify that, in her mind.

"Please give us your rank and authority," began Kingsley.

"I am a Captain in the South African Police Force and I'm in charge of the Security Police here in Durban," replied Du Toit in a clear, forceful voice.

"Was the accused detained on your instructions?"

"Yes," replied the witness. "After receiving and considering certain reports of his subversion, I instructed Sergeant Erasmus, who is on my staff, to detain the accused in terms of Section 6 of the Terrorism Act."

"Can you tell us when you first saw the accused?"

"Yes of course. It was the afternoon of the day he was detained. I believe that was the 3rd of November, 1973."

"Please tell us what happened," directed Kingsley.

"Well," began Du Toit, "I asked the accused to answer a few questions but he refused to do so. He assaulted Warder Van Zyl who was present at the interview. In fact I saw him try to strangle the Warder."

"What happened then, Captain?"

"Two of my men overpowered the accused and he was forced to let go of the Warder," he answered, glancing at Philemon. "I reprimanded the accused for this foolish behavior, and asked him again to answer some questions. He said at this point that he needed to think a bit and so I had him returned to his cell."

"That was the first time you met the accused, Captain. When did you see him again?"

"The following day when he was again brought to my office. I asked him to answer some questions and again he refused. Sergeant Erasmus tried asking him some questions too, but again he refused. So I sent him back to his cell."

"Captain," asked Kingsley, "was Warder Van Zyl present at the second meeting?"

"Yes he was, but nothing happened between them on that occasion," replied Du Toit. "That was the last time I saw the accused until after he attempted to murder Van Zyl. I did, of course, receive reports from time to time."

"Thank you, Captain Du Toit. No further questions, M'Lord," said Deon Kingsley Q.C. as he sat down.

"Mr. Griffin?" queried Judge Hughes.

Al rose quickly, smiled, and asked permission to approach the Bench, along with the Senior Prosecutor. The three conferred in undertones and then, as the Judge raised one eyebrow and lowered his head, the other two returned to their seats.

Judge Hughes lifted his head and looked stern once more. "Permission is granted for Mr. Marais to conduct this cross-examination for the Defense, as the witness is Mr. Griffin's father-in-law."

Stifled laughter erupted in the gallery, but Captain Du Toit stared at the floor in front of him. Finally, pursing his lips and ignoring Alan, he looked up into the gallery. He was sure Helena would be there and wanted to see her face, but all he could see were people laughing.

"Silence in court!" shouted the Clerk, and immediately there was a hush.

Captain Du Toit thought he just caught a glimpse of his daughter as he heard his name being called by David Marais. Reluctantly he turned to face the attorney.

"Captain Du Toit, why did the accused refuse to answer any of your questions during your first interview with him?" asked Dave.

"He was being unco-operative."

"Is it true that he refused to speak without his attorney present?"

"That's what he said."

"Did you arrange to call his attorney?"

"Definitely not. In terms of the Terrorism Act, he was not entitled to an attorney."

"I see," mused Dave. "And so you continued to interrogate him despite his protestations?"

"Most certainly I did. The Terrorism Act allows it. This is my job, Mr. Marais, whether you like it or not."

"Yes, I understand, Captain," agreed Dave and then changed his line of attack. "This building that the accused was housed in, was it what you would call a normal prison?"

"Yes," answered Du Toit, but now he was on his guard, "except that it was used only for the detention of political prisoners."

"And the procedures used by authorities in this prison, were they also normal procedures?"

"Yes, the same as at any other prison in the country."

"Is it normal procedure in other prisons to interrogate a prisoner without an attorney present, if he so requests?"

"No. That would not happen because after a normal arrest we can't interrogate a prisoner who demands an attorney."

"On the second occasion you saw my client, Captain, did he request an attorney again?"

"Yes."

"And yet you continued to question him," commented Dave in an astonished voice. "Not only that, you let him be taken away and questioned by your subordinates! Why?"

"Because I was too busy to do it myself," snapped Du Toit.

"I see, but why did you allow further interrogation when you knew such a procedure was not normal?"

The Captain looked scathing and exasperated. "Because the accused had not been detained under normal procedure. He was detained under terms of the Terrorism Act."

"So what I hear you say is that normal procedures were not used with Philemon?" asked Dave innocently. "Do you agree?"

"I suppose that is correct."

"Now Captain, on the occasion of your first interview with the accused, why did he assault Warder Van Zyl?"

"How would I know?"

"I put it to you that the accused merely retaliated. Warder Van Zyl hit him first. Can you deny that?"

"I don't know about that," answered the Captain evasively. "I was looking at some papers on my desk at the time and I only looked up when I heard shouting. That's when I saw the accused trying to strangle Van Zyl."

"Are you sure he was trying to strangle the Warder? Was he not possibly trying to push him away?"

"Oh no," replied Du Toit emphatically. "I saw his hands clasped behind Van Zyl's neck and he was using the chain from the handcuffs across Van Zyl's throat to choke him."

"The accused was handcuffed?" asked Dave, looking puzzled. "Is that normal procedure?"

"If we think the prisoner is dangerous, yes."

"But you had just met my client for the first time," said Dave aghast. "How could you think he was dangerous?"

"Because I'd read reports about him," muttered the Captain.

"Did these reports record my client committing any acts of violence?"

"He had incited other people."

"Answer yes or no Captain. Is there any record of the accused committing an act of violence?"

"If he has incited other people, he is dangerous."

"Yes or no, Captain. Any record of acts of violence committed by my client?"

"No."

"Then why was he kept handcuffed?" persisted Dave.

"Probably because his size intimidated my men," grunted the Captain.

"Captain, from what you have just told us, is it possible that the accused only assaulted Van Zyl in self-defense?"

"I've told you that I didn't see what happened. I can't answer that question." His voice was no longer as forceful.

David turned to the Judge and with a bow, quietly said, "No further questions, M'Lord." He sat down and nodded to Al.

In the spectators' gallery, H.A. closed her eyes and squeezed back tears as the full horror sunk into her. She felt emotionally numb. "How can that be the same man I loved so much as a little girl? How could he know about such cruelty and then come home and be a Dad. He must have a split personality," she thought. She cringed as she heard someone behind her mutter, "what a bastard," and wanted to disassociate herself with her father. She was grateful that nobody knew who she was.

"Any re-examination, Mr. Kingsley?" asked Judge Hughes.

"No thank you, M'Lord," replied the Q.C., half rising.

The State's next witness was Stephanus Erasmus, who duly took the Oath, proceeded to the witness stand and faced Deon Kingsley. The Q.C. stood ready to lead his witness with his thumbs hooked pugnaciously in the pockets of his waistcoat.

"Are you a Sergeant in the South African Police, stationed with the Security Police in Durban?"

"Yes, I am sir," he replied.

Al leaned towards Dave and muttered under his breath, "This one's a big brown-noser." They looked at one another knowingly, and then focused their attention on the witness.

"Can you tell us whether the previous witness, Captain Du Toit, is your commanding officer?" questioned Kingsley.

"Yes, sir, he is."

"And acting on his instructions, did you detain the accused at his home?"

"Yes sir."

"When was that?"

"On the 3rd November, 1973."

"Did the accused give you any trouble at the time you detained him?"

"No, not really, sir."

"Was that the first time you'd met the accused?"

"Yes, it was. But you see I had been keeping him under surveillance for some time before that, although I'd never spoken to him before."

"I see," said Kingsley, tugging at his pockets. "When did you see him next?"

"That same afternoon in Captain Du Toit's office. The accused was brought in there under guard."

"What happened at that meeting?"

"The Captain asked him some questions which he refused to answer. He became very hostile and tried to strangle Warder Van Zyl."

"Please go on."

"Well, some of the men in the office pulled the accused off Van

Zyl and the Captain told prisoner Dlamini what a stupid thing he'd done. The Captain then asked him some questions again and the accused asked for some time to think about it. The Captain agreed to this, and the accused was returned to his cell."

"When did you see him again, if ever?" asked Kingsley.

"The next day, sir."

"And what happened this time?"

"Much the same thing, sir. He was brought to the Captain's office and again refused to answer any questions. He was taken back to his cell."

"Was Warder Van Zyl present?"

"Yes, sir."

"Was there any trouble on this occasion?"

"No, sir, none at all."

"When did you next see the accused, Sergeant?"

The policeman glanced at his notes before replying, "Two days later, sir, on the 6th November."

"Those notes you are reading Sergeant, what are they?"

"These are the notes I took during the various interviews I had with Philemon Dlamini," he replied, holding up a small notebook.

"And will you please tell us what happened during your interview with the accused on the 6th November?" requested Kingsley.

"I went to the prisoner's cell, accompanied by Warder Van Zyl and two other Warders. Once again the accused was very unco-operative. I questioned him at length, but most of the time he didn't say a word. Warder Van Zyl pointed out to him that it would be better for him to answer us, but he was very rude and ignored us. Eventually we left him alone in the cell and went away, as we could make no progress. It's very difficult in cases like this."

"During the interview, did anything unusual happen between the accused and Warder Van Zyl?"

"Oh yes, sir," replied Erasmus, again consulting his notes. "Van Zyl was standing close to the accused at one stage, and once again the prisoner attacked him. He hit the Warder in the stomach and winded him. Fortunately the two other warders overpowered the accused before he could do any more damage."

"Am I right in saying that you only saw the accused one more time prior to the incident when Warder Van Zyl was stabbed?" asked Kingsley, turning over a page from the notes lying on the Bar.

"Yes, sir, the following night. That would be the 7th of November."

"What happened on that occasion, Sergeant?"

"Nothing at all, sir. I have virtually nothing in my notes, not because I didn't take any, but there was nothing to report. Philemon refused to co-operate."

Turning to address the Judge, Deon Kingsley bowed and said, "No further questions, M'Lord."

Mr. Justice Hughes looked surreptitiously at his watch and then asked, "Any questions, Mr. Griffin."

Alan Griffin jumped to his feet, and acknowledged his intent to cross-examine Sergeant Erasmus. He stared hard at the witness and then began. "During his evidence, Captain Du Toit stated that the prison in which the accused was housed was like any normal prison in every way, except that it housed only political prisoners. He stated that all procedures used were the same as in any normal prison. Would you agree with him, Sergeant?"

"Yes," the witness answered swiftly.

"Sergeant, when the accused refused to answer questions, did he give a reason for his silence?"

"No. In fact as I mentioned before, he was very rude and didn't even bother to reply at times."

"That's strange," pondered Al, "very strange. The Captain stated that the accused refused to answer questions because he didn't have an attorney present."

"Maybe he did, but I never heard him."

Al looked hard at him and dropped his voice, "Are you hard of hearing, Sergeant?"

"No."

"What was the question, Mr. Griffin? Please speak up, I can't hear you," queried the Judge, amidst subdued laughter in the courtroom.

"M'Lord, I asked the witness whether he was hard of hearing," replied Al.

"Apparently not," snorted the Judge. "Carry on."

"Sergeant, during your first and second interviews with the accused in the Captain's office, was my client handcuffed?"

"No."

A murmur spread through the court. "Silence!" shouted the Judge. "I will not allow this court to sound like a market place." There was immediate silence.

Alan continued, "If he had been handcuffed, you would presumably have recorded that in your notebook?"

The sergeant shifted uneasily in the witness box. "Yes, I think I would have."

"Please check in your notebook and see whether you mention handcuffs, Sergeant."

Erasmus was relieved to put his head down and fumble with his book. He was wary of Alan and unsure what the Captain had said. Finally he looked up and said, "No, not on those first occasions."

"From your reply, I presume he was handcuffed on other occasions. Is this correct?"

"Well, yes," agreed Erasmus reluctantly, "on other occasions, yes."

"Sergeant, am I correct in saying that the Captain only saw the accused during those first two interviews in his office?"

Erasmus frowned and looked suspiciously at the attorney. "I don't know about that. He might have seen him on other occasions that I don't know about."

"The Captain stated that he only saw the accused twice, and that was during those interviews," Alan informed him.

"Well, then, there's your answer."

"But the funny thing is, Sergeant, the Captain said that on both those occasions the accused was handcuffed."

The witness turned appealingly to the prosecuting team hoping for a glimpse of guidance, but both men had their heads bowed and refused to look up at his gaze. He looked at Alan Griffin with confusion all over his face.

"Well, Sergeant," pressed Al, "what do you say to that?"

Sweat was forming heavy beads on Erasmus's forehead as he murmured, "Maybe I was wrong."

"Then your notes aren't very reliable, are they?" Al shot the question like a bullet.

"No, I suppose not."

Al persisted relentlessly with his questioning, like a pit bull not letting go of its victim. "During the first interview in the Captain's office, why did the accused suddenly attack Van Zyl?"

By now the Sergeant was thoroughly confused, not knowing what the Captain's evidence had been. He attempted to be evasive, saying, "Who knows? I suppose Van Zyl might have annoyed him."

"Come on, Sergeant, you can be more accurate than that," Al encouraged him, "Didn't Van Zyl assault Philemon first?"

"Well, I er...."

"Yes or no, Sergeant. Did Van Zyl assault Philemon first?"

Erasmus coughed softly and looked at Al's penetrating gaze as the attorney waited for an answer. "Yes," he responded curtly.

"Now, Sergeant, think very carefully about what happened before you answer this question," advised Alan. "On the second occasion in the Captain's office, was Philemon badly assaulted again?"

"Yes, he was," Erasmus almost whispered, and then after biting his bottom lip he muttered almost to himself, "Why did the Captain say that?"

The Prosecutor objected, but Alan ignored this and smiled victoriously at the witness. "The Captain never said it Sergeant, you did."

Erasmus went scarlet and said something under his breath that could not be heard as such an uproar filled the courtroom. This time the Judge made no effort to quell the disturbance, but attempted to be heard above the noise. "Court will adjourn until ten o'clock tomorrow. Mr. Kingsley, please see that your witness is instructed not to discuss this case with anyone."

As the Judge made for his Chambers, Al and Dave gave one another high fives and made their way to the Dock, where they managed to shake hands with a smiling Philemon before he was led away. They watched him disappear and Al turned to Dave, nodding his head thoughtfully, "We've only won a battle, my friend, not the war."

"It was an important battle, though," smiled Dave. "Come on, find your wife and I'll buy you both a drink."

Helena had felt great pride watching Al and Dave at work, impressed by their concentration to detail and their quick-wittedness. She was thankful that schools were still on their Christmas break so that she had been able to watch the whole day's proceedings. It had been a revelation for her. The sight of her husband in such a commanding role gave her excited pleasure, heightened by the contempt she felt towards those in the witness stand. All she had heard revolted her and, as she listened, she made a resolve to make amends for the sins of her father. Remembering Al saying that evil would flourish if good people did nothing, she felt shame recollecting her momentary wish to live quietly, minding her own business. It wasn't enough to be teaching white children in a whites-only school, even though she was attempting to open their minds. She knew that she was diligent about pointing out the injustices amidst which they all lived, and it was rewarding when they responded with compassion.

"But I can do more to make a difference," she told herself, under her breath. "It's not just up to the law to change things. As a teacher I can do more too. Something has to be done about it," she said, and was startled by the person in the next seat agreeing with her very strongly.

Not realizing that she had been talking out loud, she nodded an acknowledgement and kept her musings to herself. The last thing she wanted was to engage in conversation with a stranger. She knew that there was a school run by volunteers that operated at the Catholic Cathedral on weeknights. Mary Atkinson taught black students there, and had recently suggested that Helen join the teaching team.

"I know it'll be hard work having an extra load, but I have to do it," she thought. "So much wrong has been done here without white people giving it any thought. When you hear about these dreadful things happening though, you can't walk away from your conscience. I'll phone Mary tonight and start teaching as soon as they want me."

Chapter 22

It was very relaxing, after the day's activities, to sip beers in the courtyard of the Royal Hotel and feel a semblance of normality return to their disrupted lives. It was a balmy evening and it was pleasant to be surrounded by the cheerful chatter and laughter of people whose lives seemed to know no troubles at this moment in time. Reluctant to return just yet to the nightmare of the trial, H.A. . suggested grabbing a bite to eat at the Omelet Bar.

"Good idea, but do you mind if Dave and I discuss a little bit of our strategy for tomorrow while we eat?" asked Al. "Then we can call it a day and go home. We'd better try and get a good night's rest."

It was dark outside by the time they finished their meal and made their way back to the parking garage. As they ambled and chatted along Smith Street, they caught glimpses of Durban Bay in the gaps at street crossings. It lay a few blocks to their right and, except for a large ship reflecting its twinkling lights in the water, the blackness of the bay contrasted sharply with the bright city lights around them. The rush hour was long over, but the nightly revelry had begun and the city wore a different face. The Playhouse Theatre, quaintly Tudor in design, beckoned moviegoers with the lure of Julie Christie, but only after the censors had made her latest release acceptable for white South Africa. Neon lights flashed their messages on every building except the somber City Hall, which maintained an air of propriety, like an elder statesman.

When they reached the alley that housed the parking garage, their laughter abruptly stopped. They were startled by the sudden darkness and noticed several streetlights had been broken, with shattered glass lying underfoot. It looked forbidding. The only light in the alley came from its junction at the top with Smith Street, and at the bottom from the windows of the parking garage. Between the light sources lay two hundred yards of darkness and broken glass.

Alan remembered his visit to Kwa Mashu and felt a similar sense of unease, having the same mental debate about retreat versus perseverance. He tightened his grip on Helen's elbow, saying, "Let's get a move on, I don't like this." Hearing a noise ahead of them, he glanced up in time to see three figures step stealthily out of a doorway towards them. One shape seemed very large and lumbering, and hovered behind the others.

"Hurry up," he repeated more urgently.

A gruff voice called out of the darkness, "Just hand over the briefcase Griffin, and nobody will get hurt."

"You must be joking," exclaimed Al, trying to see the dark forms, "there's nothing valuable here."

"Then you won't mind handing it over," was the reply. "Throw it down in front of you and you can walk away."

"Bloody hell! If you want it, you'll have to come and get it," shot back Al. Then he whispered to Dave, "As soon as they get close enough to reach, I'll tackle them. You take Helen and the briefcase and get out of here as quickly as you can."

"No," hissed Dave, "you'll need my help."

"Don't be a bloody fool, they won't hurt me. It's the briefcase they want. Just get H.A. out of here and back to the light."

"Alright, you've asked for it," threatened the voice in the dark. Two figures started to close in on them and the third hung back, watching.

"Go back with Dave, H.A." whispered Al. "Don't argue. Just run when he moves."

Then it all happened very quickly. Trying to give H.A. and Dave a chance to escape, Al thrust the briefcase into his partner's hands and leapt at his assailants with a savage scream, taking them by surprise. Obviously used to street brawling, the two figures in front sprang apart and turned on him with fists flying. Al turned sideways and kicked with his right leg, feeling it connect on a kneecap. He kicked the shape again and heard a satisfying crack, as his assailant fell to the ground. Then he swung around to deal with the figure that was chasing after Helen and Dave. With horror he saw the pursuer take a predatory leap and bring the pair of them to the ground, but at the same time he heard movement and wheezing behind him. The third thug, although very slow on his feet and labored with his breathing, was trying to give his downed accomplice time to return to the fray. Al turned and dodged, feeling a stinging blow land on his right ear. Automatically his right arm shot out and punched the large face looming at him. He saw his opponent fall down heavily, with breath hissing from his clenched teeth.

Helen and David, meanwhile, were in desperate trouble. H.A. had grabbed the briefcase after they'd fallen, in order to free Dave's hands for defense. This caused their assailant to pick Dave up and shove him aside, slamming him into some garbage cans that fell clattering in all directions. With Dave out the way, he lunged at Helen, punching her squarely in the nose with a loud crunch. He continued to pummel her face for good measure, before grabbing her hair and dragging her a few yards. Here he proceeded to hammer her head against a wall with sickening thuds.

"You keep to your own women and leave ours alone, you bastards," he shouted. With that he let her drop and grabbed the briefcase, all the while continuing to kick her face and prostrate body as he screamed, "Bloody commies, you're all chicken shit."

Dave came running and launched himself to defend Helen, kicking the attacker in the groin but ducking too late to avoid a fist slamming his left eye. Both men collapsed, one clutching his genitals, the other clawing at his face.

Suddenly the whole scene was illuminated as a car swung out of the parking garage and screeched to a halt. Amidst confused shouting, the three assailants took off as fast as they could and disappeared into the night. In a rage, Al started out in pursuit, having noted that in the light from the car, two of the shapes looked very like Van Zyl and Erasmus. He stopped in his tracks, however, when he heard a soft groan. Helen lay slumped sideways against a wall, with her head falling back like a broken doll. Blood poured from her mouth and nose, and her eyes were closed.

"Oh God, Helen," he sobbed, picking her up and cradling her in his arms. She lay very still.

"You shouldn't have moved her," a strange voice said, "but let me check her."

"Piss off," shouted Al.

"Don't be a fool, man, I'm a doctor. There's no time to waste here. I've just pulled out of the garage this minute. Let me take a look now," he ordered. Taking charge, he felt Helen's pulse and said, "It's very weak. Let's put her in the back of my car, it'll be quicker than waiting for an ambulance. We'll get her straight to hospital, but I'd better take a look at this other one, too."

Al caught his breath as he saw David stand up. Blood was pouring down his face and he held a hand over his eye. "Don't worry about me," he muttered, "the bastard smacked me in the glasses, that's all. Let's just get Helen to hospital."

They raced to the Emergency Section at Addington Hospital, which sat incongruously on the fun-filled beachfront, five minutes away. It seemed proof to Al of a phrase that kept coming hauntingly to his mind, "In the midst of Life there is Death." Helen still breathed though, and he was not going to let Death claim his bride.

The staff went into action quickly and efficiently. Orderlies from the Emergency ward wheeled Helen's broken body at speed to an operating theatre, while Al and Dave sat in line in the Outpatients' reception area. Before long they were ushered to different rooms where they had their needs attended. Soon afterwards, Al was released with a simple dressing on his ear and shown to a lobby where he sat and awaited news of Helen's condition.

Presently, the doctor who had rescued them, approached Al. "Your friend says that he's involved in a big court case with you tomorrow. I think you'd better make some other arrangement. There's nothing seriously wrong, but Mr. Marais isn't going to feel like a day in court."

Al nodded. "What about my wife? What's happening?"

"I don't know, Mr. Griffin, I've been removing glass from Mr. Marais." He looked at him sympathetically and added, "I'll see what I can find out."

Al got up and paced nervously, waiting for some information. Life without her was inconceivable, and waiting without knowing anything was unbearable. He felt helpless and enraged simultaneously, slapping the wall murderously in front of him. He thought of Philemon and understood the lust for revenge. "I'll get those bastards," he thought to himself, "and if Helen dies, they will die too."

An eternity later the doctor emerged with one of the operating surgeons, who introduced himself as Dr. Adams.

"How is she?" asked Al anxiously.

"She's maintaining a steady heartbeat, Mr. Griffin, but she's very weak. She lost a lot of blood, so we've given her a transfusion. We've done everything we can for her and now we'll just have to wait and see what happens. She's broken two ribs and several teeth, but she's also sustained very severe head injuries. Her face is pretty badly kicked-in, and her nose is broken. We can't tell yet whether her brain has been damaged as well as the skull, so it's hard to say what her recovery will be." He reached out and touched Al sympathetically. "I'm sorry."

"She can't die," gasped Al. "She can't."

"She's young. That helps. And it appears that before this incident, she was strong. That helps too." He paused, while looking for words. Finally he said, "You do realize Mr. Griffin, that this is a police matter and I have to report it. She was assaulted."

Al snorted with disdain and looked wearily at the Surgeon. "It's a police matter alright. Whom do you suggest we report it to? She was assaulted by the police!"

The two doctors looked in disbelief. "What did you say?" asked Dr. Adams.

Al sank wearily into a chair, put his head in his hands and felt the tears streaming down his face. "Do whatever you have to with the police. It won't make any difference. Just save my wife," he pleaded.

****

Captain Du Toit awoke to the shrill ring of the telephone next to his bed. He grabbed the receiver and muttered, "Ja, Du Toit here."

Engela Du Toit lay quietly in the bed beside him, wishing his work didn't call him out at night. She heard him catch his breath as he listened to the caller, and glanced at her watch. It was almost two o'clock.

"Where is she now?" she heard him say.

Quickly turning on the light, Engela sat up in bed and looked anxiously at her husband. His bottom lip was quivering uncontrollably as he murmured, "We'll come right away." Replacing the receiver in a daze, he gently put his arms around his wife and buried his face in her hair. Almost in a whisper, he said, "My dearest, our daughter's been in an accident. She's seriously injured. Come, get dressed quickly, we must go to her. She's in hospital."

From the time he answered that telephone call, Captain Du Toit's life became a nightmare without the relief of awakening. He and his wife drove blindly to Addington Hospital where they were ushered into a small, dark, private ward in the Intensive Care Unit. Everything was silent except for the clicking of machines and the deep exhalations of Alan Griffin, sleeping deeply on a couch in the adjoining lobby.

The Captain quietly closed the door and stared hard at the form lying in the bed. As his eyes grew accustomed to the half-light, he saw that his daughter's head was swathed unrecognizably in bandages, and what was visible of her face was raw and red. Plastic tubes seemed to go in and out of her body, her swollen eyes were shut, and she lay deathly still. His hand automatically reached for her hand, but there was no response to his touch. He was aware of his wife on her knees beside him praying, but his own knees wouldn't bend and his heart could not pray. He simply stood and stared at his daughter, willing her back to consciousness. But his will was not done.

In time the room grew lighter as dawn broke and spilled through the window. Engela looked at her watch with disbelief. It was only three hours since the fateful phone call, but she'd grown old in that time. She and Fanus Du Toit stared in disbelief at the full horror of their daughter's condition that daylight revealed. Gone was that bright, pretty face, and in its place was a combination of disfigured, unidentifiable features and broken teeth and bones. None of her beautiful hair was visible - just bandages. The Captain had seen similar atrocities at the prison, but this was his daughter and he was numb with horror.

Dr. Adams arrived, and in hushed tones explained how three unknown, white assailants had attacked her in a dark alley with her husband and another man. He was happy to tell them that her two companions had only very minor injuries, but re-iterated that Helena was in critical condition. "We're hopeful that she will come out of the coma, but we can't tell how badly the brain has been damaged at this point."

"Do you mean she might be a vegetable?" gasped Engela.

"Well, that would be the extreme and it is possible. We might be fortunate and find that she is only temporarily disorientated, having no recollection of her past for awhile."

"When do you think she'll regain consciousness?" asked Du Toit.

"It's impossible to say. Just be patient." Dr. Adams smiled sympathetically and assured them that everything possible was being done for her.

As the Captain watched his daughter again, he felt anger welling inside him. He thought of what the doctor had said, and cursed Alan Griffin and David Marais. "What sort of bloody husband is he who escapes unhurt, leaving his wife to take a battering? On top of everything else, he's a coward."

A vague hope began to grow in him that Helena would realize her husband's shortcomings and leave him. As time passed, this desperate hope became more and more realistic to him, until finally he believed that even in her unconscious state, Helena had made this decision already. He felt he had his daughter back. With this firm belief, he was finally able to pray with his wife for their daughter's recovery.

A nurse quietly interrupted their vigil to tell Captain Du Toit that there was a call for him. He ignored the still-sleeping Alan Griffin outside and made his way, with shoes squeaking on the linoleum floor, to the matron's office.

The caller proved to be Sergeant Erasmus. "I'm sorry to disturb you at such a time, sir," he apologized.

"What the hell do you want now?" demanded Du Toit angrily.

"Well, sir, I have a police report in front of me regarding the attack on your daughter. Griffin and Marais have made statements that the assailants were after their briefcase, and they allege that persons working for the Security Police attacked them. Griffin says that one of the attackers called him by name."

There was a long silence as Captain Du Toit digested this information. Eventually he cleared his throat and inquired, "Have you any knowledge about this Erasmus?"

"It's possible, sir, I can't really say," came the reply.

"Damn it, Erasmus, what the hell have you done now? Listen, you bloody fool, before you mess things up even more, just keep your mouth shut. Do you hear? If you open it, be sure it's only to deny all allegations." With that, he slammed down the receiver.

The irony of the situation was not lost on him as he returned to Helena's bedside. The Security Police, if it were true, had missed their target and hit his daughter instead. It hadn't been his command, but he knew he'd given similar orders before. He had led by example.

She looked so frail and lifeless. His only daughter was just hanging onto life. It was a sorry thing for any parent to upset the normal course of things and outlive their child. That alone was unbearable grief. But to have been indirectly responsible for this interruption was more than anybody could bear. Oblivious of all around him, Captain Du Toit went down on his knees and begged forgiveness from God and Helena. He covered his eyes with his big hands and wept.

"Oh God," he cried to himself, "she knew something that her old father forgot somewhere along the line. She tried to tell me and I ignored her. All life is sacred because you made it. Dear God, have mercy and spare her. She's too young and good to die.

"Helena, forgive me and don't let go of life my darling. You've been holding on so well, don't let go now. I want to tell you how sorry I am."

He remained motionless on his knees for a long time with his head buried beside his daughter, until eventually he became aware of the door opening behind him. Expecting it to be a nurse, he stood up to be out of the way, never taking his eyes off his child. But there was no bustling movement, only a dreadful silence. He turned and looked into the eyes of Alan Griffin. He flinched at the hatred he saw there, and not a word was said.

Eventually Alan greeted Mrs. Du Toit in a strained voice, and turning his back on the Captain, he embraced Helen's mother comfortingly. Overcome, she put her arms around him and wept.

"Why the hell didn't you protect her?" barked Du Toit finally. "What sort of man are you?"

Alan spun around with unleashed venom. "You despicable bastard. You put your thugs on us and ask why I don't protect her. What sort of man are you?"

Du Toit glared.

"I have never understood how an ogre like you could produce someone like Helen," continued Alan aggressively.

"Please stop it," begged Engela standing between them. "They'll ask us to leave if you make so much noise."

The commotion stopped abruptly at that moment as they heard a faint whimpering from the bed. Their heads turned in unison. Not one of them moved, not daring to believe what they hoped. They watched with bated breath. Again they heard a tiny murmur. As they watched, Helen's eyes opened slightly and blinked at the unaccustomed light, making several attempts to focus. She whimpered again and then made a valiant attempt to focus on some point straight ahead of her, unaware of those watching her struggle.

Du Toit rushed to the far side of the bed and took her hand, thanking God for answering his prayers. He caressed her hand with tears streaming unashamedly down his face. "My angel, you've come back to us," he whispered.

Helen's gaze moved towards him, without moving her head. She stared expressionlessly and then slowly moved her head the other way, withdrawing her hand weakly from his.

Alan stood on the other side of the bed watching her. He bent down and gently kissed her exposed face, almost afraid to touch her for she looked so frail. Choked with emotion, he tried to smile. Her eyes immediately warmed with recognition and she reached weakly towards him.

Tears poured down Mrs. Du Toit's face as she watched the couple embrace. Finally she kissed her daughter on the forehead and said, "It's good to have you back." As Helen looked at her, Engela added softly, "I love you, Mrs. Griffin! You need to rest, but I'll be right here if you need me."

H.A. tried to say, "Thanks Mom," but no sound came out. She closed her eyes again, but there was a hint of a smile on her swollen lips as she drifted back to sleep.

Alan didn't move from her bedside immediately, but Engela quietly took the Captain by the arm and led him out to the lobby. She volunteered to find them some coffee and left him brooding in a chair.

He felt confused and sat there at length, musing, trying to evaluate what had happened. He couldn't accept that his daughter had purposely turned away from him at that moment of awakening. He shuddered, remembering the look on Alan Griffin's face that revealed so much love for his daughter. He pictured again those frail arms reaching for her husband, and he winced, feeling totally excluded. He played the scene over and over in his mind, and felt nausea as he saw Alan emerge from the ward, look at him with raised eyebrows, and stride off down the passage.

"Dammit, I must try to speak to her again. I think I know what happened," he told himself, "she didn't recognize me! Dr Adams said she might have some loss of memory, and that's what happened." And then something else occurred to him; Griffin and Engela were standing in the light, whereas he was kneeling in the dark. Maybe she couldn't even see him. "I must go back," he decided.

He opened the door with renewed purpose and vigor and sped to her bed. The nurse had tilted the bed so that Helena reclined, half-sitting, and undoubtedly saw her father as she opened her eyes slightly. He caught his breath and was filled with confusion once more. She saw him, but said nothing - just stared.

"Helena," he whispered in a strained voice, "it's me, your father." He waited for some response, but there was none coming. He leant forward and added, "Remember?"

"I'll never forget," she said finally, in a rasping whisper. "Look what I have to remind me."

"What do you mean?"

She tried to shape sounds with great difficulty, and eventually uttered, "Your men did this to me."

"Helena, no," he gasped. "I know nothing about it my angel. I would never hurt you for the world."

She strained to speak. "But you let this happen to other people, like Philemon. What's one more body to you?"

"Don't say that Helena, please. If this was the work of the Security Police, I will find whoever was responsible and deal with them. There'll be an inquiry. They won't get away with it. I promise."

She closed her eyes wearily, and murmured, "There'll be others to take their place."

"Helena," he began, not knowing quite what to say, but trying desperately to gain ground with her.

He got no further. She opened her eyes and whispered coldly, "Please go away. There's nothing more to say."

"I won't leave you like this; I can't," he implored.

She turned her head away from him and closed her eyes with finality.

Fanus Du Toit gazed at her for a long time as she feigned sleep, and then he walked slowly out the door, a broken man.

Chapter 23

Alan and Dave entered court the next morning with dressings covering parts of their heads and black robes covering their bodies. At ten o'clock, when everyone was in their right place and the Clerk of the Court had called the case of the State versus Philemon Dlamini, Mr. Justice Hughes stared at the Defense Team in silence, and then quipped, "Mr. Griffin, did you and Mr. Marais have a disagreement over the conduct of this case?"

"No, M'Lord," Dave said, as he stepped forward, "I wish that's all it was. However, our injuries were sustained last night when three thugs set upon us and tried to take away our papers relating to this case. Fortunately, they didn't succeed in that. However, my colleague's wife is in critical condition in hospital as a result of the attack, and so if it pleases M'Lord, I will lead the Defense today."

Deon Kingsley leapt to his feet in protest. "M'Lord, I object to the insinuation that the State played a part in trying to deprive the Defense of its documents. I demand that my learned friend withdraw his accusation immediately."

"I most certainly will not withdraw anything I said," replied Dave. "At no stage did I accuse the State of having a hand in the attempted robbery, but if my learned friend wishes to read such an inference into my statement, he's at liberty to do so."

"Gentlemen, gentlemen," called the Judge, "Let's not start out like this. I think you are being a little too sensitive, Mr. Kingsley. Mr. Marais, you have permission to appear for the Defense. Mr. Griffin, I am sorry to hear about your wife. Now, gentlemen, if you are ready, let's proceed with the case."

Dave nodded at Al as they sat down. "Just needed my spare glasses and I'm as good as new. They're not going to get us down." He turned his attention to the court and all else vanished from his mind as he focused on the witness, standing in the box, awaiting further questioning.

"Yes, Mr. Marais," called the Judge and Dave rose to his feet again.

"Sergeant Erasmus," he began in a conversational tone, "apart from the times that you saw the accused in the Captain's office, am I correct that you only saw the accused when he was handcuffed?"

"That's correct."

"Now, Sergeant, between the last interviews in the Captain's office and the first interview with the accused in his cell, was he examined by a doctor?"

"I don't know."

"Sergeant, apart from Captain Du Toit, aren't you the senior staff member at this prison?"

"No. Warder Van Zyl is senior to me."

"I see," said Dave amiably, "but in fact because of your position with the Security Police, you would be able to give Warder Van Zyl orders, wouldn't you?"

"I suppose so."

"And you would also have access to any prison records?"

"Yes."

Dave pressed on. "Did you read those records?"

"Yes."

"Well then, according to the records, did a doctor examine the accused before your first visit to him in his cell?"

"Yes."

"Why did a doctor examine him?"

"To see what injuries he had, I suppose."

"And what injuries did he have?"

"If I remember correctly, I think he had general bruising and two broken ribs."

"And these were as a result of the assault on him?"

"Oh no, sir. I believe he fell down a flight of stairs while being escorted back to his cell."

"Is that so?" said Dave, feigning shock and confusion. "Tell me, Sergeant, on the day that Van Zyl was stabbed, was the accused again examined by a doctor?"

"Well yes, sir. You were also there during the examination."

"Yes, that's right, Sergeant. What injuries did the doctor find on that occasion?"

"The accused was still bruised. He also had badly swollen ankles and I think I remember that his wrists were cut."

"Did the same doctor perform both these examinations, Sergeant?"

"Yes, he did. He also examined Van Zyl after he had been stabbed."

"Now, Sergeant, how was the accused injured the second time? Did he fall down another flight of stairs?"

"No. He fell down the same stairs."

A murmur broke out in court and Dave demanded, "The same flight of stairs? That's a coincidence. How many times did the accused fall down that flight of stairs?"

"Just twice, sir."

"So, Sergeant, you are telling me that the accused fell down a flight of stairs twice and injured both his ankles, both his knees, cut both his wrists, and broke two ribs?"

"According to the doctor's report, that is correct."

"Sergeant, I put it to you that my client never fell down any flight of stairs. I put it to you that those injuries were sustained from sadistic torture carried out by Van Zyl in your presence."

As Erasmus, looking stricken, began to deny this accusation vehemently, Deon Kingsley leapt swiftly to his feet and interjected, "M'Lord, I object to the Defense's statement. It is quite unfounded."

"Yes, Mr. Kingsley, I agree. Mr. Marais, please refrain from making such unfounded accusations."

"Yes, M'Lord," said Dave with a small nod. His point had been made though, and he turned again to the papers on the Bar in front of him. He selected one of these papers and confronted the witness once more. "Sergeant, you have said that both the Captain and Warder Van Zyl pointed out to the accused the futility of his refusal to co-operate. Would you say that the method of pointing out was a little too violent?"

"No, sir."

"Do you mean that you feel the violence was justified?"

"No, I mean that there was no violence. They just spoke to him."

"No violence at all, hmm?"

"No, sir."

"What about the assault on the accused that you've already admitted to?" snapped Dave.

"Yes, but that wasn't when they were pointing out to him how stupid he was being."

"How many times was the accused assaulted?"

"Just once."

Dave replaced the piece of paper, picked up another and stared hard at the witness. "Sergeant, this room at the end of the corridor where the accused's cell was situated, what is it used for?"

Sergeant Erasmus looked quite reassured. "The room to which I think you're referring, is a storeroom."

"No, Sergeant," countered Dave, "I'm not referring to any storeroom. I mean the room that's fitted with electrical shock equipment, batons and a large concrete bath."

"There is no such room in the prison."

"Then if the accused says that there is such a room, which is where you interrogated him and Warder Van Zyl tortured him, he would be mistaken?"

"Yes," Erasmus said, with a defiant thrust of his chest.

"Sergeant, why was the accused kept hanging from the ceiling by a rope tied to his handcuffs?"

"He was not, sir," replied Erasmus, heatedly.

"And if the accused says he was?"

"Then he's lying." Erasmus turned and stared at Philemon in the dock, who shook his head and returned the stare. Looking back at Dave, Erasmus continued confidently, "In fact there's nowhere in the cell where the rope could be attached to the ceiling."

Dave took a step forward with his head angled quizzically. "But Sergeant, I never said this happened in the cell."

"Oh, I see, well it didn't happen anywhere else either," he answered uncomfortably.

"I intend to ask the court to permit an inspection of this prison of yours, and we'll see what the truth of the matter is." Dave turned and bowed to the Judge, saying, "I have no more questions, M'Lord."

There was a brief hum of exchange in the court as Dave returned to his seat, but it stopped immediately the Judge turned to the Prosecution and said, "Mr. Kingsley, you may proceed."

Deon Kingsley rose swiftly and nodded, "Thank you M'Lord. I call as next witness for the State, Warder Van Zyl."

All eyes were focused on the new witness as he hobbled into the court. Two months of recuperation had left him weaker, but undiminished. His stomach still strained at the shiny buttons of his uniform. He took the oath in a surprisingly small voice for such a large man, and then sneezed very loudly and blew his nose like a trumpeter, practicing scales. He appeared bruised around the right eye, with a big Band-Aid covering his temple. Al and Dave looked at one another knowingly, and nodded.

Deon Kingsley waited patiently for this to finish and then began to lead his witness. "Mr. Van Zyl, what is your occupation and rank?"

"I am a Warder of the Department of Prisons, attached to the Security Police here in Durban. I am a Warrant Officer," was the reply.

"Are you in fact, Senior Warder at the prison in Durban, under the command of Captain Du Toit?"

"Yes, I am."

"Warder Van Zyl, was the accused one of the prisoners in your charge?"

"Yes, he was."

"When did the accused come into your custody?"

"May I refer to the official records?" asked the Warder.

"Yes, please do."

Len De Villiers, Kingsley's assistant, picked up a large book from the Bar and handed it to the witness. Van Zyl studied it before replying, "I first saw him on the 3rd November 1973, when he was brought to prison by Sergeant Erasmus. He was put in cell C17."

"And what time was that?"

"Very early, five o'clock in the morning."

Van Zyl's evidence went much along the lines of the previous two witnesses, but the Warder did emphasize that the accused had taken every opportunity to assault him. "It was always me he went for and none of the others. He said things like, 'don't get too close to me, or else.' But it was always me he picked on." When Kingsley asked what he had inferred from that, the Warder added dramatically, "I thought he meant to kill me, sir."

There was a buzz of reaction as the Prosecutor continued, "Did you fear for your life?"

"That's a bit difficult to answer," said Van Zyl. He looked across at Philemon, and then back at Deon Kingsley. "I suppose I was a bit nervous of him, and if I hadn't had guards with me, I would've been scared. I'm a big man, but as you can see he is very large and threatening. Yes, I was afraid that he would try to kill me."

"Now, Warder," Kingsley continued, "what happened when you went to the accused's cell on the 8th November?"

"I pulled back the bolt and opened the door. As I stepped into the cell, I saw him crouched against the far wall and before I could get out of the way, he lunged straight at me. As he flew through the air, I momentarily saw something glinting in his hand. I suppose it was the knife. Anyway, he knocked me over and I fell on the floor where he pinned himself down on me. The other two Warders grabbed hold of him and pulled him away. The last thing I remember is looking down and seeing the hilt of a knife sticking out of my stomach and blood pouring out of me." Looking perplexed, he added, "Funnily enough I felt no pain."

Kingsley paused for dramatic effect. At length he asked gently, "I know this is upsetting for you, but can you tell us what happened after that?"

"I don't really know. I don't remember anything more until Christmas Day when I woke up in hospital." The Warder blew his nose very loudly again and stuffed the handkerchief into his pocket with difficulty.

"Thank you very much Mr. Van Zyl. It's been a difficult time for you and I appreciate your co-operation. I have no further questions." Kingsley bowed and returned to his seat, confident that this witness would not crumble easily.

"Gentlemen, before Mr. Marais begins cross-examination, I think this is an opportune moment to take lunch," said the Judge. "Court will adjourn until two o'clock."

Lunch did not exist for the Defense team. While Al sped to Addington to check on his wife's condition, Dave was able to arrange for Philemon to be left in the court with him during the recess, while armed guards were stationed outside at the exits to the courtroom. After explaining to his client what had ensued the previous evening, Dave explained that he needed help in comparing the evidence of the three witnesses. He ruled lines on a page to make four columns, heading each of these in turn; Du Toit, Erasmus, Van Zyl and Philemon. The evidence of each was quickly jotted down in their respective columns, and finally Philemon was asked to give his comments for the fourth column. "Anything you can think of," Dave urged him, " no matter how small and unimportant it seems to you."

"Why don't you just take the Judge to see the prison? It's all there for him to see," asked Philemon.

"Yes, you're right. We intend to do that, but at the moment all that would prove is that Erasmus lied when he said the torture room did not exist, and we already know that he's a liar. Besides, what do we do if they've hidden the evidence? I don't believe they're going to leave too much on display."

"They can't hide most of this stuff. It's built in!"

"We'll get there soon, but what we must do now is try to shake Van Zyl's calm demeanor and then fire questions at him. If we can make his evidence suspect; if we can make the doctor agree that your injuries could not have happened as they say they did; if we can get Van Zyl to admit that he could have possibly stabbed himself as he fell; then we will be in a good position to prove your story by exposing the torture chamber to the Judge. Trust me."

Philemon smiled. "I do. You've both risked much for my sake. Let's get to it then." They put their heads together and worked at the comparison chart, knowing that it would speed up the cross-examination of Van Zyl, and that if he were not telling the truth, with questions coming fast at him, he could easily get confused and allow something vital to slip.

Al arrived back just as they were finishing, feeling much relieved that Helen had regained consciousness and had spoken briefly, but lucidly during his visit. He'd had difficulty concentrating on the case all morning, but he just had time to look over their notes before policemen came to return Philemon to the dock, and the afternoon session began. He was able now to focus all his attention on the case.

With instruction from the Judge to do so, Dave rose to begin his cross-examination. He stared hard at the witness, trying to get the feel of the man, and asked, "Mr. Van Zyl, have you ever served as a warder at any other prison?"

"Oh yes. I've been with the Department of Prisons for twenty-one years now, but I've only been with the Security Police for the last two years."

"And the other prisons where you served, were they normal prisons?"

"I don't know what you mean," replied Van Zyl, cautiously. "The prison I'm at now is a normal prison."

171

"Let me put it this way, would you agree with Captain Du Toit and Sergeant Erasmus that the only difference between this and other prisons, for example Durban Central Prison, is that your present one houses only political prisoners?'

"That is correct."

"So apart from this, do you consider it a normal prison, employing normal procedures?"

"Yes, I do."

"Well then," demanded Dave, "why did you allow one of your prisoners to remain handcuffed the whole time he was in your custody?"

"I did not," snapped the witness.

"Oh really! Captain Du Toit and Sergeant Erasmus claim that each time they saw the accused, he was wearing handcuffs."

"Yes, but not on my orders," countered the Warder.

"Who gave those orders?"

"Sergeant Erasmus. When he first brought the accused to my prison, he gave orders that the handcuffs were not to be removed without his permission."

"Oh I see. And tell me Warder, did the Sergeant or anyone else ever order the handcuffs to be removed?"

"Not to my knowledge."

"So the probability is that whilst the accused was in your custody, his handcuffs were never removed?"

"Yes."

"Can you explain to me how the accused could have stabbed you if his hands were handcuffed together?"

"Well, he ... er, he just kind of had the knife in one hand and put both his hands out in front of him." A bead of sweat appeared for the first time on his forehead and he reached into his pocket for his handkerchief.

Without pausing to allow the witness to regain his composure, Dave continued, "Mr. Van Zyl, can you describe this knife that stabbed you?"

"I can't really, no. It went in so deep that I only saw the hilt sticking out of my stomach. That's all I saw of it."

Dave walked over to Kingsley, picked up a knife lying on the Bar, and showed the weapon to the witness.

"Is this the knife?"

"As I said before, sir, I can't swear to it."

"Well, the State will lead evidence to the effect that it is the knife that stabbed you."

Van Zyl shrugged and the corners of his mouth turned down. "Then I suppose it is."

"It's not a kitchen knife, nor one that the accused might have stolen from his food tray, is it?"

"No, definitely not. Prisoners aren't given any knives with their food," he said with a look of scorn.

"Where could the accused have obtained the knife then?"

"I don't know. They smuggle weapons and drugs, I don't know how. We watch them like hawks, but they still do it."

"Philemon had no visitors while in prison, nor did he come into contact with any other prisoners. Am I correct?"

"Yes."

"And he was searched by one of your warders before he was put in the cell?"

"Yes."

"Were you supervising this search?"

"Yes."

"And did he have such a knife on him?"

"No."

"Then can we accept that when he was first put in the cell, the prisoner didn't have the knife with him?"

"Yes."

Dave continued relentlessly and carefully. "And am I correct in presuming that nobody ever went into the prisoner's cell except in your presence?"

"Yes."

"And you never saw the doctor or anybody else hand him a knife?"

"Certainly not."

"I put it to you that he got the knife from you, Mr. Van Zyl."

"That is ridiculous!" exclaimed the witness. "You think I gave him a knife to stab me?"

"Not intentionally," said Dave, "but when you threatened him with the knife, he swung across the room on the rope by which you had him hanging from the ceiling, and he kicked you to defend himself. You collapsed with the knife still in your hand and that's how you were stabbed. You fell on your own knife."

"No," Van Zyl cried, sweat pouring down his face, "you're wrong. He had the knife, not me."

"But how could he have tried to stab you when his hands were tied above his head?"

"He wasn't tied up like that, I'm telling you. He had his hands tied together in front of him but he wasn't hanging from the beam."

"What beam?" snapped Dave.

"You said he was hanging from a beam."

"No I didn't, Mr. Van Zyl, I used the word ceiling, not beam."

With a face red and streaked with sweat, Van Zyl looked fearfully at the attorney. He tugged at the collar of his uniform, which had grown exceedingly uncomfortable.

"Well, Mr. Van Zyl, what do you say to that?"

All eyes were riveted on the Warder, who blew his nose again and said, "I must have misheard you. My ears are blocked up with this cold I've got. I'm sorry."

"Oh I don't think you misheard me. The accused will say in evidence that he was left suspended by his hands from a rope, flung over a beam in his cell."

"He's lying, sir, there is no such beam in his cell."

"We'll see." He stared at the witness and then turned to study his papers again. The silence increased the Warder's tension. Suddenly Dave looked up and shot at him, "Did you take a doctor to the accused's cell?"

"Yes."

"Why did you do that?"

"I had orders to have him examined because he'd been injured when he fell down some stairs."

"Who gave these orders?"

"Sergeant Erasmus."

"Now that is strange. Sergeant Erasmus said in his evidence that he'd only learned about a doctor examining the accused, by looking at prison records. Are you lying under oath?"

"No," Van Zyl replied indignantly.

"One of you is lying," Dave continued calmly.

"Well it's not me."

"Mr. Van Zyl, the accused will say that he received his injuries, not from a fall down stairs, but from a brutal assault by you and your guards."

"He's lying. I'm not on trial, he is. And he's the one who's lying," shouted the witness, his voice gaining strength as his temper frayed.

Dave continued his remorseless cross-examination. "I think Sergeant Erasmus would say that you are lying. He told the court that you assaulted the accused."

"I don't believe you," was the stunned reply. "I am not on trial here. You can't speak to me like this." He turned and appealed to the Judge, "He can't, can he Your Honor?"

While this examination was going on, Justice Hughes was leaning forward intently in his chair, as one who has to strain to hear. "Just answer his questions, Mr. Van Zyl. I'll stop him if he asks anything improper," he responded without emotion.

Dave nodded. "Now why did you assault the accused?"

"I did no such thing," the witness exploded.

"So then Sergeant Erasmus is a liar?"

"Yes."

"How many men helped you to hold the accused under water in the concrete bath?" asked Dave, changing his line of questioning suddenly.

"If Erasmus told you that, he's lying," he screamed.

"Just answer the question, please."

"Nobody held him under any water."

"And what were the names of your men who beat the accused's legs?"

"Nobody did that to him. He fell down some stairs. I saw him fall. Actually he fell twice."

"How did you know what injuries he sustained?"

"The doctor told me."

"When you took the doctor to see him, how many times had he fallen?" asked Dave.

"Just once."

"When did he fall again then?"

"I think it was on the 7th November," replied Van Zyl.

"But you said that the doctor told you that the accused had injured his legs," snapped Dave.

"When I was in hospital he told me."

"I see, after you'd regained consciousness on Christmas Day?"

"Yes. That's right."

"Did you see the accused fall the second time?"

"Yes."

"Then can you tell us how he cut his wrists?"

"He caught them in the railings of the banister. He was handcuffed, you see, and the handcuffs got caught in the railing as he fell. It stopped his fall with a jerk and cut his wrists. They bled quite a lot."

"I must congratulate you on an ingenious reply, Mr. Van Zyl, but my client will say in his evidence that he never fell down stairs at all. I put it to you that his injuries were caused from being beaten remorselessly by your men."

"That's not true."

"I put it to you that he received cuts on his wrists from handcuffs cutting cruelly into his flesh when he was suspended by a rope, hanging from a beam in his cell."

"That's a lie."

"Isn't it true that you teased and threatened him with a knife while he hung from that beam?"

"No."

"And when he kicked and swung to defend himself, that's how you were stabbed?"

"No! I've told you how it happened," cried Van Zyl.

"Did you enjoy torturing him with electricity and watching him writhe in agony?"

Deon Kingsley leapt to his feet. "M'Lord, I object to this line of questioning. There has been no evidence of electricity being used."

"Objection over-ruled, please continue, Mr. Marais," muttered the Judge.

Dave nodded to the Judge, "Thank you, M'Lord." He turned again to the witness, saying, "Then what did you do to make him talk?"

"He never talked," said Van Zyl with exasperation.

"Nevertheless, what did you do to try and make him talk?"

"Nothing, I swear."

"Where did you interrogate the accused?" demanded Dave, changing the focus of his attack once again.

"I never interrogated him, that was not my job. I was just the warder. Sergeant Erasmus was the interrogator, and also Captain Du Toit. But mainly, Sergeant Erasmus," he replied, mopping his brow.

"And where did the interrogation take place?"

"In the Captain's office."

"Are you quite sure the interrogation didn't take place while the accused was hanging in his cell?"

"I've told you, that never happened."

"Was he interrogated in his cell at all?"

"No! I'm telling you it took place in the Captain's office."

"And was the Captain present?"

"Yes, twice he was."

"Mr. Van Zyl, Sergeant Erasmus says that apart from those two occasions, the interrogations took place in the cell."

"Well he's wrong about that."

"Everybody seems to be wrong except you," exclaimed Dave, raising his eyebrows.

"All I'm trying to tell you is that the Sergeant made a mistake.

Maybe he forgot or something." Van Zyl's large frame was beginning to sag dejectedly.

"Then I presume he made a mistake in his notes as well!"

Exhausted, but pleased with the lengthy cross-examination, Dave turned slowly to the Judge and said, "No more questions, M'Lord."

Judge Hughes felt drained of energy. It was imperative that he keep an open mind to both sides of the argument and show no bias. He had heard many tales of horror and brutality in court, some true and some not, but what he had heard today sickened him and he was glad that the truth would emerge, one way or the other. He sensed that there would be grueling days ahead, and, needing time to study the proceedings of the day, he announced that court would adjourn until the next morning. Thankfully he retired to his chambers.

Chapter 24

The following day Helen drifted in and out of sleep, sedated and weak, but off the critical list. Next to her bed were bouquets of flowers and rows of cards from well-wishers, and she noticed them with pleasure at moments when she opened her eyes. Sometimes she discovered that Al was there on awakening, and she tried hard to concentrate staying awake, talking to him and then falling asleep still dreaming about talking to him. It was comforting to know he was there. Her mind seemed to have emptied itself of much that had happened in the last few days and the doctor had explained that this was Nature's way of protecting the brain from trauma.

Her mother was often there too, sitting patiently next to the bed and just smiling when Helen looked at her. "You're getting stronger all the time," her mother assured her. "Just rest and keep it up, my angel." When she dreamt of her mother, Helen always saw them together surrounded by flowers, and waking or dreaming, it was difficult to differentiate now. It all seemed surreal.

Hearing a slight rustle, Helen opened her eyes to see a nurse next to her bed with another bowl of flowers, fragrant yellow roses. She placed them carefully on the trolley and handed an envelope to H.A.

saying, "This came with it."

Left alone, Helen began to read the note that she recognized to be in her Father's writing. Soon her eyes were swimming with tears.

Darling Helena,

I have always found it difficult to express in words what I feel, so please bear with me. Firstly, I want to tell you how overjoyed I am that you are on the way to recovery. You are very precious and we had some dark hours when we thought we'd lost you. Thank God you have not been taken from us.

Thank God too, that He gave me such a daughter. You have challenged my conscience and made me do much soul-searching. You have your mother's goodness and you have made me realize that all life is sacred and that I have abused it. Please forgive me, Helena.

I have always told you that one of the most difficult things a person can do is to face their mistakes and make amends for them. I want you to know that I have resigned from my post in the Security Police. I could not continue.

God bless you.
Your loving Pa

She cried uncontrollably for some time, overcome with love for him. Then she reached for the telephone next to her bed and dialed.

"Du Toit here."

"Pa...."

"Helena?"

"Thanks for the flowers, and God bless you too."

Chapter 25

The world's press watched and listened carefully as the third day of the trial began. Journalists hovered like vultures, sensing the scent of decay and awaiting the moment they could descend to gorge. How much rot would emerge?

As he was marched from the police van into the court cells, cameramen from around the world frantically photographed Philemon. The crowd seemed divided in its sympathies. Some stood disdainfully watching the controversial figure, having already judged him a communist and would-be murderer. Their loathing was visibly evident. Others, however, shouted encouragement and stretched out to touch him as he strode past. Here and there in the crowd, he saw faces he knew; there was John, his old drunken friend, smiling a brilliant smile of encouragement; and there was Reverend Mkize calling out, "Have faith." His eyes scanned the crowd for a glimpse of Simon Gumede, but he couldn't find him. Then he was out of the sunshine and into the gloom of the court.

The Judge seemed tense as he took his place on the Bench, and a sense of anticipation filled the room. Everyone realized that the trial had probably entered its last lap as Deon Kingsley, Q.C. rose to call his next witness. Dr. Johannes Meyer took the oath and, with the help of the senior prosecutor, gave an impressive list of his qualifications that clearly marked him as an expert witness.

"As the local district surgeon, what are your duties?" asked Kingsley.

"Among other things, I examine and report on suspects who've been detained by the police, such as drunken driving cases. From time to time I'm called to examine and report on prisoners who've been injured whilst in custody, for example if they've been injured in a fight."

"In the course of your duties, have you ever examined prisoners at the political prison in Durban?"

"Yes, a few times," acknowledged the doctor.

"And have you ever examined the accused?" asked Kingsley, pointing to Philemon standing in the Dock.

"Yes, I have."

"When was that?"

The doctor opened a folder that he had taken into the witness box with him. After studying the contents for a short while, he replied, "The first time I examined him was on the 5th November, 1973."

"Where did you examine him?"

"In his cell."

"Was this in the political prison in Durban?"

"That's correct."

"Doctor, can you tell us what you found during your examination of the accused?"

There followed a detailed and technical explanation of the concussion, bruising and broken ribs. "I recommended hospitalization for the accused," he added.

"Doctor," continued the Q.C., "were you informed of the cause of the injuries?"

"Yes, I was. Warder Van Zyl informed me that the accused had fallen down a flight of stairs."

"Were the injuries you've just described, consistent with that?"

"Yes, I would say so."

"Can you tell us what happened on the morning of the 8th of November, 1973?"

"I was called to the prison and taken to the accused's cell where I found Warder Van Zyl lying on the floor with a knife protruding from his upper abdomen. I gave him a brief examination and an injection. When Captain Du Toit arrived, I told him that Van Zyl needed to be hospitalized urgently, and an ambulance was ordered. I accompanied him in the ambulance."

"Did you examine the Warder at hospital?"

"Of course. He was rushed straight to the Emergency Operating Theatre where I worked with a medical team to save his life."

"Please tell the court about his injuries."

The Doctor described how the knife had penetrated and pierced the Warder's spleen and liver, and how bacteria from the wound had caused a grave infection to race through his body, raising his temperature to a dangerous level. He had also fallen very heavily because of his immense body weight, and banged his head so hard on the concrete floor that he had damaged brain tissue. He concluded that the Warder was extremely lucky to be alive.

"Were you told how the knife came to be in his upper abdomen?"

"Yes, Captain Du Toit explained."

"Would you say that the injuries you have described were consistent with a stab wound?"

"Of course they were," retorted the doctor. "I told you that I saw the knife in his abdomen and I later removed it myself at the hospital. Warder Van Zyl was stabbed."

Kingsley picked up the knife that was lying in front of him and handed it to Dr. Meyer. "Is that the knife?"

The doctor examined it momentarily and said, "Undoubtedly."

Kingsley turned to the Judge and said, "I hand this in as an exhibit M'Lord," and then turning to the witness again, continued, "When next did you see the accused?"

"That evening. Captain Du Toit called me to examine him and I again recommended hospitalization. He was bruised and cut. I believe the Captain acted on this, and admitted the accused to King Edward."

"Were you told how the injuries had occurred?"

"The Captain informed me that this man had fallen downstairs again."

"Was anyone else present when you examined him?"

"Well, there was the Captain of course, as well as Sergeant Erasmus. The two attorneys for the Defense were also present." He gestured towards Dave and Al.

"Thank you, Doctor," concluded the Prosecutor, returning to his seat.

The Judge glanced up from his notes and asked, "Any questions, Mr. Marais?"

"Yes, M'Lord," David replied, pushing his chair back and standing up with a sheaf of papers in his left hand. He placed them on the Bar in front of him, pushed his glasses up on his nose and began his cross-examination.

"Doctor, you said in your evidence that the first time you examined the accused, his body was covered in bruises, his face was lacerated and he had two broken ribs which were broken in the front, not the back. He also had severe bruising at the top of his spine and the base of his skull. Is that correct?"

"Yes."

"Doctor, the evidence before the court is that when you made your first examination of the accused, he had only fallen once. Bearing this in mind, let us try to work out how he sustained these various injuries while falling down a flight of stairs. Would you say that the general bruising on his body was a result of him rolling down the stairs after he tripped and fell to the floor?"

"Yes, that's probably right."

"Do you agree with me that it is a natural reaction when falling, to put one's hands out to protect oneself, or break the fall?"

"Yes, indeed."

"Well now, Doctor, if a person's hands were tied in front of him, presumably if he were to fall backwards he would be unable to use his hands to break the fall?"

"Correct."

"Now, remembering that when the accused fell, his hands were tied together, would...."

Suddenly Kingsley, realizing where the line of questioning was leading, jumped to his feet and interrupted. "M'Lord, I object. This witness is a doctor and an expert in the field of medicine. He can describe the injuries to the court and he can give an opinion on what caused them. More than that he cannot do. If my learned friend wants to establish how the accused fell and at what angle the body hit the floor, he must call an expert in that field."

"Mr. Marais, do you wish to reply?"

"Yes, M'Lord. I submit that the Doctor has common sense, which is all that's required here, not an expert in the field of falling down stairs! Surely he can say whether a person whose hands are tied in front of him can break his fall if he falls backwards?"

"Yes, I agree. The objection is overruled. Please proceed."

"Thank you, M'Lord," said Dave, turning back to the witness. "Now where were we? Oh yes, Doctor, if a person falls backwards down a flight of stairs, at a time when he cannot break his fall, would it be possible for him to sustain such bruising at the base of his skull that it could cause concussion?"

"Oh yes, indeed," replied Dr. Meyer, "especially if he hit his head on one of the steps."

"And this person falling in the way I've described, would it be possible for him to sustain lacerations to his face and to crack two ribs? Would it be possible to sustain severe chest injuries with a fall like this?"

"Well, the lacerations to the face could quite conceivably have been caused when rolling down the stairs. But the chest injury is puzzling, because the initial force of the fall would have been spent on the back." He frowned and rubbed his forehead for a moment, before adding, "He's a very big, heavy man though, and so I cannot exclude the possibility that the weight of his body did injure his chest whilst he was rolling downstairs."

"Doctor, let me ask you this. Were the accused's injuries consistent with a severe beating?" inquired Dave cautiously.

"It depends," came the equally cautious reply.

"On what?"

The Doctor looked ill at ease. "Let me say that it would depend on what was used to beat him."

"I see. Well let's say for example, the butt of a rifle was used, wielded by a large man about the size of Warder Van Zyl."

Kingsley was on his feet immediately. "M'Lord, I object to the insinuation made by the Defense."

"Yes, Mr. Kingsley," agreed the Judge. "Please refrain from this practice in your questioning, Mr. Marais."

"M'Lord, I apologize. Let me rephrase that. Were the accused's injuries consistent with a severe beating with the butt of a rifle, wielded by a very corpulent man?"

Suppressed laughter was heard in the courtroom and the Doctor looked down at his hands to control his facial muscles. When he looked up, he once more looked inscrutable. "Yes, they could have been caused that way," he conceded.

"Doctor, you said in your evidence that you recommended hospitalization for the accused?"

"That's right."

"To whom was this recommendation given?"

"Warder Van Zyl."

"What was done about it?"

"Nothing."

"Nothing!" echoed Dave incredulously. "You mean to say that here was a man who needed hospitalization and nothing was done about it?"

"I'm afraid so. I could do no more than make a recommendation."

"Doctor, which version do you prefer, the one where the accused fell down a flight of stairs, or the one where he was beaten?"

"I really can't say."

"Why not?"

"Because both versions are plausible."

"Can you tell us when you examined the accused in his cell, what furnishings did you see there?"

"There was nothing, just a blanket."

"And what was the floor made of?"

"Concrete."

"Did you notice the ceiling? Can you tell us what it was like?"

"No, I'm afraid not. I don't recall looking up at all."

"Was the accused handcuffed when you saw him?"

"Yes."

"And was he lying on his blanket?"

"Yes."

"Did you give the accused any injections while you were there?"

"Yes, I gave him morphine."

"Surely you looked at the hypodermic against the light?" Dave prodded.

"I suppose I did, but I don't recall noticing anything other than the syringe."

"Were you angry that your recommendation to hospitalize the patient was ignored?"

"Yes, I was furious, but there was nothing I could do about it."

"Surely you could have insisted?"

"It wouldn't have helped. I know it wouldn't, it's happened..." The Doctor stopped abruptly. "You see," he began again, "it's a prison, not a hospital, so I can't order anything, only recommend."

Dave leaned forward aggressively. "Were you about to say that it's happened before?"

The Doctor sighed deeply and nodded his head. "Yes."

"Who told you about the accused's injuries, Doctor?"

"Warder Van Zyl."

"Before or after the examination?"

"Before. I like to get as much information as I can."

"When was the next time you saw the accused?"

"On the 8th November, at about nine o'clock in the evening. I remember it was late."

"Had he sustained any further injuries or obtained any further treatment since you'd last seen him?"

"Yes and no. He was further injured in that his knees and ankles were severely swollen and both wrists were cut and bleeding. But his wrists had been bandaged, rather inexpertly."

"Was he still handcuffed?"

"No."

"Did you see me there?"

"Yes, you and Mr. Griffin and Captain Du Toit were all there."

"Did we get an opportunity to talk to you?"

"No."

"Who told you how the accused obtained the second lot of injuries?"

"Captain Du Toit."

"When did he tell you this?"

"After the examination."

"Not in front of Mr. Griffin and me?"

"No. When we were alone, later."

"Doctor, he had the opportunity to tell you that information when you entered the room and he got up to shake hands with you. He was obviously trying to prevent Mr. Griffin and I contradicting him with the accused's version of how he had sustained those injuries. That would seem to be the reason for his disclosure after we had left, wouldn't you agree?"

Kingsley was on his feet instantly. "I object to that question," he thundered. "The witness could not possibly know what was on the Captain's mind."

Dave nodded courteously, confident that he'd made his point despite withdrawing the question. Turning again to the witness, he pressed on with his attack. "The damage to his knees and his ankles, Doctor. Could he really injure them so badly falling down stairs?"

"I suppose so."

"Or could the injuries possibly have been sustained by a constant hammering on them with rubber batons or tjamboks over a long period?"

The Doctor gave a suppressed start. "Yes, they could have."

"And when you examined the cuts on his wrists, did they look like the result of a sudden jolt from getting caught in the banister, or did they look more like they had been caused by long and constant rubbing of handcuffs?"

"I would say that it looked more like rubbing than a sudden jolt had caused the cuts, but the handcuffs were not tight and chafing, so...."

"But if he had been strung up with a rope through the handcuffs, keeping him off the ground, his whole weight would have been hanging from his wrists. Would that have done it?"

"If that were so, yes, that could've caused the injuries to his wrists."

"Doctor, after your examination this second time," Dave continued relentlessly, "did you recommend to the Captain that the accused be hospitalized?"

"Yes."

"Had his condition deteriorated since you'd last seen him?"

"Definitely."

"When was the accused sent to hospital?"

"The following day, November 9th."

"Wait a minute, I'm confused. Help me here a minute. You saw Warder Van Zyl on the morning of the 8th of November?"

"Yes."

"At what time?"

"It was between ten and eleven. About tea-time."

"What!" exclaimed Dave. "You saw the Warder at tea-time but you didn't examine the accused until after dinner, about eleven hours later? Why didn't you examine him immediately afterwards?"

"I do what I'm told, that's why. I wasn't asked to examine him until that night."

"So this man was left lying injured without medical attention for eleven hours. Actually it was more than that because he must've been injured before Van Zyl."

"I don't follow your reasoning."

"Van Zyl saw the accused fall down the stairs, he told us. I presume he didn't see that after he was stabbed."

"No, that would've been impossible."

"And then it wasn't until the next day that he was finally taken to hospital. It all seems very callous. Well, be that as it may, tell me this Doctor," said Dave, changing his tack once more, "do you think that the accused, in his weakened state, could have stabbed Van Zyl with enough force to damage him so extensively?"

"Yes, indeed. In an act of desperation one can do amazing things. We are all capable of increased strength with adrenalin pumping through our bodies. In certain circumstances, I have no doubt that the accused could summon superhuman strength."

"What sort of circumstances? Do you mean if he hated somebody enough and lost his temper?"

"Yes, that sort of thing."

"Well let's think about that. If the accused had been very badly abused by this person; beating, threatening, near-drowning, shocks, and then a lewd suggestion was made about the accused's wife. Would that provide that spark of anger necessary for extra strength?"

The Doctor shrugged and opened his mouth to speak, but Dave continued, "And if the accused were hanging from the ceiling with Van Zyl standing in front of him, brandishing a knife, threatening to castrate him, would that not drive the accused to make a desperate attempt for freedom?"

"But if he were tied up and hanging from the ceiling, how could he possibly try to get free?" protested the Doctor.

"Would that matter? In that state of mind, do you think he would stop to ask himself about the rationality of his action? Don't you think he would just focus on kicking that mocking, threatening face?"

"Yes, that's likely."

"So, he summons up his strength and kicks. His feet hit the Warder, who then falls. Whether the Warder falls on the knife and stabs himself, or whether the force of the kick stabs him, is irrelevant. The wound caused by the knife in Van Zyl's stomach, could it have happened the way I've just described?"

The silence in the court was absolute as everyone strained to hear the Doctor's reply.

He whispered hoarsely, "Yes, it's possible."

A collective sigh was heard from the gallery as Dave turned to the Judge and bowed. "No more questions, M'Lord."

As the prosecution did not wish to re-examine, the Judge suggested that the Defense use the half hour before lunch to address the court, as they had earlier requested. Dave declined the offer for the moment, asking instead for an inspection of the prison. "I feel it is absolutely necessary that you see this, M'Lord, so that you can really understand my client's state of mind."

"M'Lord," interrupted Kingsley. "I really don't think an inspection is necessary and will just waste the court's time. If my learned friend wants to prove anything, let him lead evidence to do so. Incidentally, M'Lord, I have been instructed to inform the court that the Government of South Africa is shocked at these allegations of torture and abhors the whole concept of extracting confessions by such methods."

Dave reached for his notes and addressed the Judge. "If I may make an observation here, M'Lord. Article 5 of the Universal Declaration of Human Rights of 1948 states, and I quote, 'No one shall be subjected to torture or to cruel, inhuman or degrading treatment or punishment.'

"What is interesting to note, M'Lord, is that at the time of adoption of this Declaration, only the Soviet Union, Czechoslovakia, Poland, Yugoslavia, Saudi Arabia and South Africa abstained from an affirmative vote. Strange bedfellows for a State that feels threatened by Communism!"

"Mr. Marais, please don't waste our time with irrelevant information. I fail to see what this has to do with inspecting the prison. Please keep to the point."

"I apologize M'Lord. The point is that if we were to inspect the prison this afternoon, we might well end the case immediately. That would save the court a lot of time. If the implements of torture are not there, then serious doubts will have been cast on the accused's honesty and reliability. On the other hand, if they are there, then the State's witnesses are being untruthful. Maybe that's what the State is afraid of," he added.

"M'Lord, we have nothing to be afraid of," countered Kingsley indignantly. "We'll see you at the prison."

"Very well, Gentlemen," ruled the Judge. "Court will now adjourn for lunch and we'll meet outside the prison at two o'clock."

Chapter 26

The summer rains had started while they'd been in court, and it was a shock to emerge and find that the morning sunshine had given way to a torrential downpour that had taken the city by surprise. The sky was dark and the rain came down in an onslaught of heavy darts. It was like two seasons in one day. All the gutters and storm drains were bubbling with fast-flowing water. A few umbrellas dotted the streets, but most people, caught unawares, either dashed bare headed or with makeshift plastic bags resting atop their heads.

Al and Dave's car sent up a wave of spray as it made its way to the Prison. The windscreen wipers worked at double-quick time and still it was difficult to see the road, increasing the tension in the car as driver and passenger brooded over the pending inspection. Al had never had any doubts about the truthfulness of Philemon's story, but he had a nervous knot in his stomach nonetheless. They arrived behind the police car bringing Philemon, and watched him being led through the rain into the building that had allegedly been the scene of so much suffering. Kingsley, De Villiers and Judge Hughes pulled up at the curb within a few minutes and they all dashed inside to begin their task.

In the lobby, Sergeant Erasmus and Warder Van Zyl stood silently waiting and watching Philemon, who was standing tensely with his armed police escort. The policemen all looked antagonistically at the visitors as they entered and after a brief, awkward silence, the Judge said sternly, "As soon as Captain Du Toit arrives, we can proceed with the inspection."

Erasmus stepped forward and coughed. "I'm sorry, sir, the Captain won't be with us this afternoon. I have been authorized to show you the prison."

The Judge looked astounded. "What do you mean the Captain won't be here? This was a court order!"

Deon Kingsley cleared his throat nervously. "The Captain is indisposed."

Mr. Justice Hughes stared in amazement at Kingsley, then at Erasmus and Van Zyl. "Extraordinary," he muttered. "Well, you'd better lead the way, Sergeant."

"Yes, sir," replied Erasmus, opening a door leading to the interior of the building and into an adjoining corridor. "If there's any door closed that you want me to open, please don't hesitate to ask," he said unctuously. "Warder Van Zyl has the keys here."

The ground floor consisted of offices, accommodation for the prison staff and a canteen. Off-duty warders were lounging around, playing cards. Near the end of the corridor was the Captain's office, exactly as described by the witnesses. The group then entered the elevator and was taken to the top floor. They stepped out into a corridor identical to the one they'd just left on the ground floor. The doors opening off it were mostly record rooms where staff members were busy filing documents.

Back in the elevator, the Sergeant pressed the third and last button, and the party descended to the basement. Here they found yet another corridor, but this one had no windows and the only light source was from light bulbs set at intervals in the ceiling. Erasmus led his visitors to a large metal door marked C17. He turned and nodded to Van Zyl, who smiled and proceeded to unlock the door. He stepped aside and Erasmus beckoned the visitors to enter. "This is the cell in question," he said solemnly.

It was a tight squeeze to fit nine people into the confined space, but it was clear to see that it contained a blanket, a metal tin and spoon, and it had a smooth ceiling.

"It's not possible," came an anguished cry from Philemon. He gazed dumbfounded around the cell and then looked at the door to see Van Zyl smirking. He yelled furiously at his captor, "You bastard, you've covered everything up."

The Defense attorneys demanded chairs to stand on, and tapped at the ceiling in many places. It was solid concrete with no possibility of false panels. They then demanded to see the interior of every cell on the floor, whether or not there was an inmate. They were all identical.

Philemon shook his head dejectedly as Al and Dave looked puzzled, trying to figure out what could have happened. "Well gentlemen," said the Judge, breaking the silence, "let's see the so-called interrogation room at the end of the corridor."

Van Zyl strutted smugly and unlocked the door, swinging it open to reveal an interior containing shelves piled with linen, blankets, floor polish and prison uniforms. "As you see, sir," said Erasmus, "it's a storeroom. Feel free to tap these walls and check if there's anything hidden behind. However, I think you'll find everything in order."

As Al and Dave made a close inspection, Erasmus commented to the Judge, "It's such a shame. If these people would only put their energy to good use, they'd keep themselves out of trouble. They make up stories about our brutality all the time. I don't know why they don't do something useful with their lives."

The Judge refrained from answering this, but muttered, "When these gentlemen have satisfied themselves here, I'd like to see the staircase in question please."

Finally, Al and Dave had to concede that this was in fact a storeroom and nothing more. Van Zyl led them to the next exhibit, a dimly lit staircase. They walked up and down, and were shown where Philemon was reported to have fallen. "This isn't true," the prisoner said desperately to his attorneys. "I never walked on these stairs once. I never even saw them. We always used the elevator. I don't know how they've done it, but they're hiding things."

"Shut up, you," shouted Van Zyl.

Erasmus quickly interjected. "Have you seen enough, sir?"

"Yes, that will be all," replied the Judge and then added, "unless there's something else the Defense would like to see." He looked at Alan and Dave, who shrugged their shoulders, too upset to speak.

They all entered the elevator and Philemon found himself staring at the gloating face of the Warder. His eyes followed expressionlessly as Van Zyl reached out and pressed the middle button, sending his mind back to another day when he had watched the Warder push the buttons. Another day, months ago. He stared intently at the big hand that had subjected him to such pain, and suddenly remembered the Warder shouting at him for staring. He looked up at the hated face and an idea rushed into his head. They were hiding something and the clue was in this elevator. As the doors opened on the ground floor, he shouted abruptly, "I've got it! I know what they did. I can show you."

"What are you talking about?" Judge Hughes was highly annoyed at this wasted time, and was not pleased at having been brought out unnecessarily in the rain.

Philemon's eyes were bright with excitement. "I think I can show you why the cell and the interrogation room were different, if I can just try the control panel..."

"This is ludicrous," exclaimed Deon Kingsley. "We've seen all there is to see and this is fabrication."

"But I know we haven't seen everything. I think there's another basement!"

There was a loud grunt from Erasmus. "What nonsense. Sir, you have seen the whole building and the prisoner is just trying to delay things. He's a nuisance."

Al interrupted, "Can you prove this Philemon?" He looked urgently at his client, then at the Judge. "Can he at least try and show us?"

The Judge nodded and Philemon quickly moved away from the restraint of his guards towards the control panel of the elevator. Van Zyl stood in his way and cursed. "He's a troublemaker, that's all. There is no other basement, I'm telling you. You're mad, Philemon. You tried to kill me and you're trying to escape your punishment. I hope you swing!"

"Mr. Van Zyl," admonished the Judge, "I've made my ruling. Now please stand aside."

Reluctantly the Warder moved away and everyone stared at Philemon as he studied the panel for a while. He was sweating and biting his bottom lip as he gingerly pushed his forefinger on the panel immediately below the bottom button. He felt the metal give and his heart gave a leap as the doors began to close. Nobody stirred as the elevator moved and ground to a halt noisily, opening to reveal an identical corridor to the one they'd just left.

"You see," said Erasmus, "we're in the same place."

"I don't think so," said Al. "It might look the same, but this elevator undeniably moved, and it moved downwards."

Philemon stepped cautiously out of the doors and walked slowly down the corridor, followed by the rest of the group. It certainly looked the same as before in every detail. Suddenly Philemon broke into a run and stopped at a door marked C17. "This is it, I know it is," he whispered hoarsely, as the others caught up with him.

"Open the door, Van Zyl," ordered Alan.

The Warder looked quickly at Erasmus, who in turn coughed and muttered, "We've already been in here. Can't you see the number? C17."

"I said open it," repeated Al.

Van Zyl slowly fumbled around in his jacket pocket, while everyone stared fixedly at him. Finally he selected a key and turned the lock with a shaky hand. He slowly drew back the bolt and pushed open the metal door.

The concrete floor was bare except for a blanket, a metal plate and a spoon; but when they looked up, their eyes met a huge beam that stretched the length of the room, just a few inches below the ceiling.

From the beam dangled a rope.

The Judge sighed, and whispered, "My God!" He put his hand on the black man's shoulder and asked gently, "Philemon, would you like to show us the interrogation room?"

He nodded and led them to the end of the corridor, where he indicated a locked door. Turning to Van Zyl, he said with sudden authority, "Give me the key."

Pushing him aside, the Warder muttered, "Cheeky bastard. Nobody touches these keys except me."

"Well, go right ahead then. Just open the bloody door," shouted Al.

Nobody spoke as the door grated open. Al flicked the light switch to reveal a table that was covered with wires and electrodes, thick chains hanging from the ceiling, and a large concrete bath. The only noise was the hum of the electric light. The stunned visitors were speechless.

****

It was a somber group that entered the courtroom to take their assigned places. The Defense team, although relieved that their client had proved his point, were in shock at the realization of what had been done to him in the name of State security. Seeing the chilling evidence was a lot more meaningful than hearing what had been done.

Justice Hughes looked ashen-faced as he entered and sat down at the Bench. He glanced at Dave and asked, "Mr. Marais, is it your intention to lead any evidence after what we have just seen?"

Before the Defense attorney could respond, Deon Kingsley jumped up and interrupted, "M'Lord, may it please you, but after viewing the evidence this afternoon at the prison, I do not believe there is a case against the accused, and with your permission, I wish to withdraw the charges. I ask your Lordship to discharge the accused."

"Mr. Marais?" inquired the Judge, glancing at David.

"In the circumstances, I join my learned friend in asking that my client be discharged," he replied.

A slight murmur rippled through the gallery and curious glances were exchanged, but silence quickly returned as the Judge began to speak. "Will the accused please stand?" As Philemon rose, Mr. Justice Hughes watched intently and his expression softened. "Mr. Dlamini, you have been abused," he began. "I will ensure that a copy of these proceedings will be forwarded to the Attorney-General's office so that the actions of the law-enforcement officers will be investigated." He took a sip of water and removed his glasses. "Furthermore Mr. Dlamini, the case is dismissed. You are free to go."

Everyone clamored to congratulate Philemon, Al and Dave at the same time. They were thumped on the backs, their hands were shaken and their names rang out through the court. The crowd could only conjecture what had transpired at the prison, but they were satisfied for now that justice had been done. Philemon was quick to move to his attorneys' sides and embrace them. Cameras flashed to capture that moment and share it next morning on the front pages of all the newspapers.

"My friends," the newly freed man sobbed, "I don't know how to thank you. My heart is very full." Tears streamed down his face as he whispered, "I've just awoken from a nightmare."

Al was close to tears himself as he said softly, "Welcome back from that nightmare, Philemon. You're a very brave man and what's happened to you will change everything. From this day onwards they will never dare do such things again. You should be proud that your suffering has saved many from a similar fate." He put a supportive arm around his client and began to steer him towards the door. "Let's get you home," he smiled.

It was not possible for Al and Dave to enter Kwa Mashu at such short notice without permits, so they called their colleague, John Ngcobo to drive Philemon home. John arrived in court with Pat Moodley, both looking very agitated. They congratulated Philemon, but then Pat quickly took Al aside, talking to him in undertones. Dave and Philemon watched uneasily as John sighed, saying, "Hate to spoil your excitement, but we have to break the news to you sooner rather than later."

"Shit!" muttered Al, turning away in disgust.

"What is going on?" demanded Philemon, alarmed. His freedom was too new to feel at ease, and the tension he observed was terrifying.

"We've just heard that the Appeal Court has thrown out the reference book cases. From now on, all Blacks have to keep their passbooks with them at all times. We're back to square one," Pat repeated.

Philemon relaxed. "Is that all? Man, after what I've been through, that's nothing. We expected that would happen."

Al looked at him incredulously. "How can you be so long-suffering?"

Philemon laughed loudly. "Because I am an African. We learn patience when we're tied onto our mothers' backs. You white people expect everything to happen instantly. We learn that we have to wait until the time is right. Patience, Al. You don't have much of it."

"My God, it's more than patience, you just accept things. You have such forgiveness and tolerance," he exclaimed.

"Yes, you're right. It's much more than patience, it's ubuntu."

Chapter 27

Mama Gloria's Eating House was the center of the universe on the night of Philemon's release. The proud residents of Kwa Mashu welcomed their leader home, their own David who'd just beaten off Goliath, and everyone wanted to talk to him or touch him. Some had to be content with merely seeing him as he sat on a hard wooden bench, surrounded by his friends from the Committee and occasionally sipping from a tin of beer.

Philemon sat close to his friend, John Msomi. They had to speak very loudly in order to hear one another. John had a great need to unburden himself, and pointed to his beer-tin. "This is the last beer I will drink, and it's only to celebrate your return, my friend."

Philemon smiled indulgently at his old friend, knowing and understanding his weakness. "This is a good thing you tell me. Today has seen many good things."

"But I want to tell you why I am doing this." He shook his head with self-recrimination. "I have caused you much trouble and it was all because of the beer. My brain became soft like an old man's when he becomes a child again. I couldn't think because I was drunk and that's when the Hyena would come to me. He bought me drinks and asked me questions. I was too stupid and drunk to know," he sobbed. "Oh Philemon, I didn't think a man would do that to another."

"Say no more, John," replied Philemon, patting the old man on his shoulder. "The Hyena is a bad man and you have learned your lesson. There are many others like him, police informers. We have to be on our guard. Where is he now?"

"He was murdered - they necklaced him."

"Hau," Philemon exclaimed, "no man deserves that. That's bad. But tell me John," he lowered his voice, "where is Simon?"

John took a long drink of beer and then deliberately pushed the tin away. "You mustn't tell anybody," he said after a long pause. "It's too dangerous to know these things."

Philemon suddenly felt cold. "What things, John?" he asked, alarmed.

"I haven't seen him for a long time, since before the fat man fell on his knife. Something happened to Simon and he started to say bad things while you were in prison." His voice was barely above a whisper and Philemon strained to hear. "He said we have to use guns if we want to change things. I said no." He stared at the table sadly. "I tried to talk to him like a father, but he got very angry and shouted at me. He said you were wrong too. He said we are old and toothless, and too afraid to change."

"So where is he now?" Philemon already knew the answer to his question, but he asked it nevertheless.

"He's gone somewhere far away to become a soldier." He stared anxiously at Philemon, and added, "I'm very afraid for him."

"Yes, I am too," agreed Philemon wearily. "There's too much violence and it doesn't work. Look what happened with me. The State used violence and what happened? The whole world knows about our suffering and now the police are the criminals. Everything will be different from now on. If only Simon had waited."

"I know," said John sympathetically. "But he was very angry and said we have to stop sitting waiting for handouts from the whites. He said we must be proud to be black, instead of trying to be like the whites. Even people like Mr. Griffin, Philemon, he said there's no place for him here."

Philemon put his head in his hands wearily and was silent for a long while. "How can he say that? There's room for all of us. There are good and bad people, blacks and whites. Would he rather have had the Hyena for a friend than Alan Griffin, just because he was black? If only he'd waited and I could've spoken to him. I love him like my own son."

"I know you do. He loves you too, I'm sure. It's because he was so angry when they took you away. He saw them do it you know, and he went to the attorneys and told them. He saved you, but he just didn't realize it. And he was very angry with me too because of the beer."

Philemon sighed. "Too much has happened John. I'm very tired now." Oblivious of his surroundings, his voice trailed off as he said, "Tomorrow I'm going home to Zululand. I want to see my wife and child. Sometimes I thought I'd never see them again." He turned and looked at John. "I was so alone."

****

Bang, bang, bang. Philemon woke with a start, sat up abruptly in bed and tried to remember where he was. Bang, bang, bang, the noise continued. Gradually he realized that he was in his room and that the noise was coming from the door. His reaction was to run, but by now the door was open and a white man confronted him

"Are you Philemon Dlamini?"

Philemon nodded mutely.

"I'm Sergeant Botha, Security Police. I have an order here, signed by the Minister of Justice, authorizing your detention. Come with me please."

Philemon felt confused, as if he were in a dream. "But I've just been released from prison. I was found not guilty of any crime. How can you arrest me?"

"Suppression of Communism Act. Now come."

He was filled with a sense of futility as he sat in the back of the police car, quite powerless. "What was the word Simon had used?" he asked himself. "Toothless. I still don't agree, but they're forcing Simon to fight with guns. I can see why he's gone away. Maybe he's right."

He looked at Sergeant Botha in the front seat and considered that he was simply another face in the mould of Sergeant Erasmus, and doubtless there would be another Van Zyl. The names would be different this time, but everything else would be the same. "I don't know the answer anymore," he thought to himself. He looked at the South African coat of arms in the police car and sighed as he read the motto, "Unity is Strength."

"What's the problem, kaffir?" grunted Botha. "Thought you'd been too clever for us, didn't you?"

"I don't think anything anymore. I don't understand what's happening."

"There's only one thing you need to understand, and that's to answer questions when we ask you. We want to know where you went when you left South Africa, and we also want to know some more about your friend, Simon Gumede. Otherwise you're going to Robben Island this time."

There was no sound but the monotonous hum of the car. Outside was a dark, African night, lit only by the beams of the headlights on the road ahead.

"You know something, Sergeant Botha," Philemon thought to himself, "you don't know what you're doing any more than I do. Your white nationalism has created black-consciousness, so there's no unity and no strength. There's hatred and fear. But we're all people of Africa, even you Botha. We need African-consciousness." He shook his head in despair. "God help us, God help Africa, we can't help ourselves." Then he closed his burning eyes and added, "God help me. I've grown old and tired and my voice has run out...."

EPILOGUE

The night seemed endless as they flew through time zones over the Atlantic Ocean. Her memories and her dreams became interwoven as Helen slept fitfully, or impatiently watched the map on the screen charting their course. As they entered African airspace, she felt a surge of excitement that swelled more and more as the arrow crossed over the border and her beloved South Africa lay beneath them. By now they could watch in the early morning light and see little dirt roads amid winding, sandy rivers. Wisps of smoke, far below, were traces of lives being lived down there. She felt shivers as she watched, mesmerized by the vast ochre plains.

Tears came to her eyes as she remembered her mother standing at the airport all those years ago, refusing ever to leave South Africa. "Your father and I go back eight generations and I'm too old to transplant now. This is where I belong, Helena," had been her litany. "We always did what we believed was right, even when it was difficult. Now there are wrongs to be put right. I must stay here, I believe your father would have wished it."

It filled Helena with resolve to vindicate her father's death. He had been a brave man of conscience, cut down by cowards. She realized that her father was the example she needed to understand reconciliation. First you have to recognize your wrong doings; then you have to repent, no matter what it takes; then only can you hope for forgiveness. Erasmus and Van Zyl had been temporarily suspended from duty while an investigation had been held. However there'd been lack of evidence to charge them when Captain Du Toit had died after his car had exploded. The police claimed that terrorists had killed him, and Erasmus and Van Zyl had been re-instated with promotion.

"I'm going to clear any dark shadows from the past," she thought to herself. "Those who knew no mercy then, will be shown none now. They can call it revenge on my part if they like, but those two men will not be granted amnesty if I can help it. They've shown neither remorse nor conscience."

****

Durban, South Africa, 2000. St. Elizabeth's Church Hall served as a makeshift court for amnesty hearings, and today the crowd was colorful and noisy at the combined hearing of Erasmus and Van Zyl. The committee, however, sat somberly at a row of tables on a raised platform, looking pained from all the harrowing details that they were forced to absorb in the course of their duties. Reverend Mkize was completely white-haired and his brow was deeply lined. The work on the Truth and Reconciliation Committee was the hardest thing he had ever done in his life, and yet he felt honored to have been asked to do it. Each new case he heard filled him with renewed horror at man's capacity for cruelty and loss of conscience.

He looked at the two men now in front of him, Erasmus and Van Zyl, and found it hard to compose himself as he stared at their hands, remembering the barbaric things they'd done with them to his old friend, Philemon. All that they had done had been well documented in the trial many years ago. They claimed that they had been only performing official duties required to interrogate prisoners, under orders from the late Captain Du Toit. They acknowledged sending a letter bomb to Mr. David Marais at his home, and expressed regret, but declared it was necessary again for political reasons, and that, once more they were only carrying out orders from Captain Du Toit. They denied, however, that they had been implicated in the death of the Captain himself.

It was at this moment that Helen Griffin stood up and walked briskly to the front of the hall. There was a curious hum as spectators observed this unknown woman. The white walls contrasted against her solemn figure, clad neatly in a dark suit. Television cameras zoomed onto her as she stood in front of the microphone, removed her dark glasses, and stared at the two men.

"Do you remember me?" she asked.

The two men looked at each other and shrugged.

"No," said Erasmus.

"Perhaps if I showed you a picture of what I once looked like before reconstructive plastic surgery, it might help." She raised a blown-up picture of herself taken on her wedding day. "The last time we met was in Devonshire Lane, just outside a parking garage. Do you remember now?"

They stared at her uneasily. A breeze stirred the air soundlessly but otherwise nothing moved. All eyes were focused on the speaker.

"It was a long time ago and it was very dark, so I can understand why you're having trouble remembering. Let me refresh your memories. Somebody had broken all the streetlights. Maybe you couldn't see too well as you tried to grab my husband's briefcase and then attacked me. Is it coming back to you now?" She cocked her head quizzically to one side. "Did you know that you broke two ribs, cracked my skull in multiple places, broke my nose and smashed my face to pulp?" She held up another blown-up photo of herself, taken as she lay in hospital. There was an audible, collective gasp at the sight of the bloodied, shattered image.

"Not nice to look at, is it?" She cleared her throat. "I'm Helen Griffin. You knew me once as Helena Du Toit."

"I didn't know it was you," whispered Erasmus. "I thought it was Marais. As you said, it was dark. I didn't know. I'm sorry."

"Does it make it any better that you thought it was David Marais? You did a good job of destroying my face, and if you hadn't been interrupted, I daresay you might have killed me." She held the photo up a few moments longer and then placed it carefully on the desk beside her. Feeling her throat constrict with anger, she took a deep breath before demanding, "And how can you say that my father ordered you to send a letter bomb to David Marais? You know my father had resigned already. He didn't have any authority to give you such orders."

"He didn't really resign. That was just a cover. He was still in charge."

Helen turned and looked at her mother, who shook her head.

"That's not true. This is supposed to be truth and reconciliation, or had you forgotten already? Truth, it's that concept you don't seem to understand."

The two men opened their mouths to speak, but neither had the chance to utter a syllable. Helen put her hands up in front of her to signal that she would not be interrupted.

"I have a letter here from my father, telling me of his resignation. You will see that it is dated prior to Mr. Marais' death. In fact it was written just after you had attacked me, thinking it was David Marais. The letter is one of my most treasured possessions because it reveals my father's decency and honor. He gave you no orders to send bombs," she continued, holding up the note her father had sent her in hospital all those years ago.

"Well the orders were given to us. It wasn't our decision."

"Who gave you orders to plant a bomb in my father's car?"

"We didn't do that. Terrorists put it there. They hated the security police. We were all in danger. You never knew when they'd attack you. It was terrible, and I'm sorry that your father died."

"Spare us your lies! My mother saw Mr. Van Zyl bending down next to the car inside the garage on the day it happened. She was looking out the window while you were distracting my father inside. At the time she didn't realize what he was doing, and it was too late when she did realize."

Van Zyl began to protest. "She's talking rubbish...."

"No! My mother has been too terrified to reveal this until recently, for fear of her own life. Attempts on two members of your family can do this to you, don't you think? And when the police had become the attackers, well - exactly where could she report the matter? But the thought of you being granted amnesty was more than she or I could tolerate. We will never forgive you. Your actions were cowardly and criminal then, and they still are. You're trying to save your own skins by blaming a dead man who can't defend himself. A man, I believe, you killed yourselves. It has always been your pattern; you attack the defenseless. You should be charged for crimes against humanity, not granted amnesty. When police and officials are corrupt, when they abuse their power as you did, society has reached its lowest ebb. It has to stop." She replaced her dark glasses and returned to her seat.

****

A small group gathered in Mrs. Du Toit's front room to be with Al, Helen and their children. Philemon and his wife, Frieda, had flown from Cape Town with their son, Nkosinati, and Simon Gumede, so that they could be present at the hearing. They all sat now with Reverend Mkize, Carol Marais (Dave's eighty year old mother), William and Hilda Griffin, and Mary Atkinson-Bold. Mary turned to Hilda Griffin, whom she had not seen since Helen and Al's wedding day, and smiled. "Your daughter-in-law did a fine job today, didn't she? Who would have thought she'd stand up to those beasts so confidently and just let them have it! Certainly not the H.A. I first knew." She hiccupped as she took a sip of wine. "I was quite terrified of her myself!"

Hilda laughed. "Oh Mary, when roused, that angelic-looking little thing is a force to be reckoned with. We discovered that many years ago. Still water runs deep, as they say!" The white haired lady, still elegant, glowed with happiness. "I am so proud of her. It's lovely to have them back. And my grandchildren, well.... what can I say? They are perfect!"

William Griffin put his arm around his wife's shoulder and agreed. "She and Alan are a great couple, and as parents we couldn't have hoped for more. It's funny how things work out, isn't it? Too often we are hasty in our judgments - but that was all a long time ago." He and his wife clinked their glasses together in a toast, and Mary added her glass too.

Suddenly Al looked at his watch and interrupted everyone, saying, "It's time for the news. Before we eat, let's quickly see what coverage we got today."

They knew already that amnesty had been denied and the case turned over to the State for prosecution, but there was satisfaction to be gained anew by seeing the proceedings in replay. They all cheered as they watched Helen on the screen and she put her arm gently around her mother, whispering in her ear, "That was for Pa."

"I know."

"What would he have said about all these people being here in his house tonight?"

Engela smiled. "Once he'd got over the shock, he would've been proud."

Philemon watched the mother and daughter, together, reconciled to all that had torn their lives apart twenty-six years ago in the dark, troubled times. He marveled at the capacity of the human spirit to endure unimaginable suffering, both physical and emotional, and to emerge with compassion and dignity. His own pain was something he never revisited anymore. "This new country of ours is trying to do that too," he mused. "There is so much pain that will never be forgotten. But we have examples of magnanimity all around us, right from the President to the ordinary man and woman in the street. We are very blessed."

"Forgiveness doesn't change the past," he would often say when invited to speak at meetings, "but it does wonders for the future. In fact, truth and forgiveness are the bridge to the future. It'll take time. It took a long time to break down what was wrong, and it's going to take time to build up something good. But we will do it - all in the fullness of time."

He leaned over to his wife and caressed her hand gently. She had been as strong as he had, with all the patience of Africa in her soul. Then he glanced at Mrs. Marais who had lost her first-born. She looked so sad and tired. "The women in South Africa paid a high price in the struggle. The suffering was felt far beyond the prison walls. We were all victims of a great evil; even those who perpetrated atrocities were victims of evil," he thought.

His musings were interrupted by the phone ringing and Helen running to answer it. They heard her laughing and speaking in Zulu before returning to call Simon. "It's your mother. She's very excited because she saw you on T.V." Helen stood in the center of the room and addressed everybody at the same time. "I feel like I'm in some sort of time warp, remembering how things were and then returning to find so many changes. It's like two different places. Mrs. Gumede has a television and a telephone! It's amazing. I feel like I've had too much champagne," she laughed.

Simon returned to the room and joined in the laughter. "My mother is very happy. Everyone in the village came to watch her T.V. and now they're all celebrating!"

"I think we should do the same. Hilda and Helena, could you help me dish up the food? My grandchildren and Mary have already put everything out on the table for us," Engela said. "Mrs. Dlamini and Mrs. Marais, would you like to help us too?"

Alan watched the diverse group and thought sadly of his good friend Dave; how excited he would've been by today's events and the new democracy he'd helped father. He could imagine Dave smiling as he pushed his glasses up his nose, and clearing his throat earnestly. He stood next to Mrs. Marais and said gently to her, "Your son was one of the finest men I've ever known, and the best friend I've ever had."

Her eyes glistened with emotion. She nodded and answered in a strained voice, "I'm very proud of him and all he did, even if I didn't understand at the time." She closed her eyes to squeeze back a mother's tears. "I miss him so much. I wish he'd emigrated with you, Alan. He'd still be with us. It wasn't safe for him here."

Alan took her hand in his. "I wish he had too. But he stayed to fight the fight here, not from afar. He was a brave man. We're all indebted to him, and to you for giving him to us."

They all huddled around Engela Du Toit's hospitable table, laden with boerekos that she cooked so well, and she looked flushed with pleasure as she invited Reverend Mkize to say Grace.

"Mrs. Du Toit, I would be most honored," he replied.

With bowed heads they listened to his soft voice begin to pray. "Dear God, thank you for this food that we have before us, so lovingly prepared. Thank you for bringing us all together in love and friendship to share it, and thank you for granting us the wisdom to do so. Please God, help Africa and all her people. Guide us to heal this land that you have entrusted to us. We ask this in your name, Amen."

Printed in the United Kingdom
by Lightning Source UK Ltd.
9806800001B/61